SONG OF THE FLESH

THE story of Ruby Wilson, whose beauty was
startling on advertising posters, but even more
startling in real life. The men who wanted her but
somehow lost her make an interesting list of
marked variety. The man she wanted but somehow
lost had a striking effect on Ruby's career. The
transformation of the girl who grew up in back of
a hat shop in a small town into a personage of note
and notoriety is the theme of a novel that takes
its realism straight. How men took to Ruby
and Ruby took to men, and how love flared
and waned in a darkened furniture
store—all is told in swift scenes
that sing clearly the song
of the flesh.

Song of the Flesh

by Ruth Cummings

M. EVANS

Lanham • New York • Boulder • Toronto • Plymouth, UK

M. Evans
An imprint of The Rowman & Littlefield Publishing Group, Inc.
4501 Forbes Boulevard, Suite 200, Lanham, Maryland 20706
http://www.rlpgtrade.com

10 Thornbury Road, Plymouth PL6 7PP, United Kingdom

Distributed by National Book Network

Library of Congress Cataloging-in-Publication Data Available

ISBN 13: 978-1-59077-496-0 (pbk: alk. paper)

♾™ The paper used in this publication meets the minimum requirements of American National Standard for Information Sciences—Permanence of Paper for Printed Library Materials, ANSI/NISO Z39.48-1992.

Printed in the United States of America

To my mother, Ida
and
To my uncle, Louis B. Mayer

I dedicate my first book

SONG OF THE FLESH

WHEN Ruby Wilson was fifteen her beauty was something startling. She was born somewhere, and raised in the back of the hat shop owned by her Aunt Carrie.

The shop stood on the corner of Dock Street, near Nicki the Greek's Fruit Market. There was a gold sign on the window . . . CARRIE WILSON, CHAPEAUX. The same black velvet hat with the jet had been in the window for five years; it was the ancient relic of a style just recently come back into vogue. It was carefully placed on tissue paper, and surrounded by a sickly pink rose, a purplish ostrich plume, and some old buckram shapes. There was a bell on the shop door and it gave a funny little tinkle whenever anyone came into the shop.

Aunt Carrie had been very careful about sending Ruby to school. She knew she'd get into trouble if she didn't. She combed out the long corn-colored hair and trimmed the bangs across Ruby's forehead.

"Go on, now—git to school—learn somethin'—make somethin' out of yourself."

"Don't want to make nothin' out of myself!"

And Ruby stood defiantly and faced the elephant woman who was her aunt. "Don't want to stay in this town and make hats all day long that nobody wants."

Aunt Carrie smacked Ruby across the face. "My trade is exclusive, Ruby! Now git to school and shut your mouth!"

Ruby pinned her dress low in front and pulled up her stockings. Then she covered herself with her aunt's toilet water—lilac. Defiantly, she flung at Carrie:

"Why don't you take that black velvet out of the window—looks like the devil!"

Her aunt was furious. She raised her two hundred and fifty pounds, well corseted and well pressed, out of her chair.

"Look here, Ruby—I brought that black velvet from Paris with me and it's going to stay in the window."

"When from Paris? Maybe thirty years ago— maybe?" And Ruby was out of the store.

Nicki heard the clinking of the bell and stood on the sidewalk in her way so she couldn't pass.

"Hello, Ruby—where'd you get that hair? Pretty."

"Let me go, you big wop!"

Nicki laughed between a smooth black moustache.

"*I*—no wop. I—Greek. Sure thing—I Greek. How you like Nicki, the Greek?" and he chucked her under the chin.

"Go on—get out of my way! You smell of garlic!"

And Ruby pushed him with all her strength. Nicki laughed, and stepped out of the way.

Ruby was not popular at school, in spite of her clear loveliness. Those attracted by her beauty were quickly repelled by her sullen manner—by the dull odor of lilac toilet water on soiled flesh. But this never bothered Ruby. She didn't want to go to school anyway.

And she wasn't going this morning. She hadn't been going for over a month. She hated school. She hated everyone. She even hated her aunt—who sat in back of the store all day sewing hats that nobody ever bought.

Ruby turned down Main Street and walked past the Empire Hotel. From the corner of her eye she could see three men seated on the black leather chairs in the window and smiling at every girl that went by. Ruby went by twice. She glanced at the red-headed man in the middle. He was very young. Then she brushed her corn-colored hair out of her eyes and walked away. The young man gave a low whistle.

"Who's the kid with the yellow hair and the big blue eyes?"

He was quickly informed.

"Ruby Wilson, the best looker in town—and temper like an alley cat. Better look out, Red—she's under age—"

Red laughed, and threw his cigar into the spittoon, adjusted his tie and sauntered out of the hotel.

"Where you goin', Ruby?"

She raised her blue eyes and stared straight at him. There was something about his slim, young, vital face that interested her.

"How'd you know my name was Ruby?"

Red laughed. "Say, I've heard about you from everyone."

Ruby answered a little harshly:

"Who's been tellin' you things about me?"

"Lots of fellas I know—said to me—when you get to St. Marks, you'll see a real beauty. Ruby's her name—but be careful!"

"I don't know no fellas."

"Go on—quit your kiddin'. But I'm not afraid of you, Ruby."

"Wait 'til my aunt catches you with me."

Red laughed again.

"You live with your aunt, eh? What's she like—anything like you?"

Ruby walked off and a sullen look came into her face. He couldn't tell whether she was going to answer him or not. Then suddenly:

"She's fat as an elephant—and makes hats."

Red took her arm. Then he laughed boyishly and his face grew almost the color of his hair.

"Listen—I got just today in this town—and I got a car. Would you like to go somewhere for lunch—and a ride—then a movie? Would you?"

Ruby sucked in her lip. She was interested.

They drove out to the lake. Red had a pint of whiskey. They stopped off at a fish place and got some sandwiches. Then they parked the car and went and sat on the sand on the shore.

"Pretty lucky me running into you like this—" and his hand fumbled with her knees.

Ruby pushed him away in a vigorous shove.

"Keep your hands to yourself! What do you think I am!"

"I think you're a pretty fresh kid—" and he ruffled up her hair and kissed her roughly. She hit him with her hand and made an ugly red mark across his face.

Red smarted with pain. Before he could grab her again, she was up on her feet and down the beach. His eyes were dark with resentment. Her husky laughter came to him and he wanted to kill her.

"Say, what's the idea running off like that? Come on back—!"

Ruby turned and looked at him, but fled. Red cursed her. His mouth was set in a hard line as he ran down the beach after her.

He called her name. In answer, a pebble caught him on the ear. It stung, and the ear bled. Ruby laughed loudly at his startled face, and threw more sharp edged pebbles at him. He turned his back trying to duck the pebbles and ran back to the car. Ruby saw him go. She dropped the stones and ran after him. But he ignored her. His temper was flaming and his lips were cut and bleeding from her playful stones.

"Red, don't go—don't go!"

He watched her running toward him along the beach, her corn-colored hair whipped from her face—calling to him. But even her loveliness had no effect on him, now.

He wiped the blood away from his mouth and ear. It covered his hand. With a violent curse he lumbered up to Ruby. She stood before him—her eyes clear and innocent, her sharp white teeth parted in a smile.

"Don't be mad—" and she touched his arm gently.

He pushed her away with a vicious shove and his small eyes were smouldering with a madness.

"Yeah—don't be mad! You crazy kid!"

Ruby smiled. It was a fragile smile. "I didn't know what I was doin'—that whiskey sure knocked me for a loop." Her voice was low and persuasive.

And Red was entirely caught in her wide smile.

"Well, cut that out. You play my way, or we're going back to town—see!"

"What's your way?"

"You'll find out—but it ain't throwin' stones and cuttin' lips, see?"

He caught her arm. "Let's go back to the sand."

They went back—back to the sand. Red wanted her now as he had not wanted her before.

They were laughing now. Her firm strong thighs were close to his and her corn-colored hair was in his eyes. He held her tight by the arm as they walked, and flashed her a warm look.

On the beach, they found a pine grove covered with cones and a large log. Red seated himself on the log and drew Ruby down beside him. His senses were filled with her.

"Gee! You're pretty, Ruby," and he brushed her hair from her eyes. "You're sure pretty. How old are you?"

"How old do you think?" And Ruby leaned back against the cones and her yellow hair was sprawled over the sand.

Red looked straight at her. "Oh, seventeen."

Ruby laughed.

"Sure, seventeen—nearly eighteen. Don't I look eighteen?"

"I don't know—maybe you do."

"How old are you, Red?"

"What's age got to do with a man! I got a big job—salesman for the biggest underwear concern around here." He looked closer at her. "But I heard you was just a baby." His eyes narrowed shrewdly: "You ever been in love?"

Ruby shook her head.

He didn't believe her. She had known love, all right. She was too pretty to have slipped by. He rubbed her stockings nervously.

"I'm pretty well steamed up about you, Ruby!"

She lay indolently on the sand and her voice was cool and lazy. "That's the whiskey—it's gone to your head."

"No, Ruby—it's nothin' to do with whiskey that makes me feel like I do." And he brushed his bruised mouth over her throat.

She pushed his face away and sat up rigid like a doll. He pulled her toward him.

"Aw, come on, honey, be nice to a fella."

She pushed him away. "Leave me alone—say, where's the rest of that bottle?"

"You had enough, Ruby—"

She slipped out of his arms; her eyes flashed; her even white teeth snarled at him.

"My aunt lets me drink all the time—she has a quart of somethin' every night. We drink it together—and sing songs. I been drinking since I was thirteen."

She stumbled to her feet and started for the car. Red watched her staggering along the beach. His small eyes glittered like sharp pins. There was something about Ruby that infuriated him. Early in the afternoon when he had seen her with her corn-colored hair walking indolently outside the Empire Hotel, there had been a strange excitement in his nerves, and he had thanked God he had no work to do that afternoon.

But Ruby was not what Red had expected. He had spent three dollars for the loan of a car, bought a pint of whiskey, and driven her to an isolated spot on the beach. For what? His nerves had tingled in anticipation of the afternoon alone with the girl. He had expected her to get drunk quickly, and with that a little amorous, and then—

He had wanted the satisfaction of kidding the two men who had sat with him in the window when he first saw Ruby. He had wanted to insinuate that she was not only good looking, but—

Red was disappointed. If he were still to make good his boast, he would have to tackle her a little differently than he had. He couldn't make her out. No other girl had ever had a will like that—a will of iron. It made him uneasy. She was not the ordinary pick-up. He was worried. Maybe she had never been picked up before. Maybe she was still a kid who had never gone off on an afternoon with a red-headed fellow who saw her from the window of a cheap hotel.

Ruby was hunting for the liquor in the car. He watched her quietly. He was a little uncomfortable. This yellow haired girl was difficult enough to manage when she had only a few drinks. He imagined she would be vicious if she drank more.

Red paused a moment and smiled. There was something exciting about the fact that Ruby might be vicious. He imagined she would bite and claw. Well, he'd knock her across the mouth if she dared—the little alley cat! That's what she was, an alley cat. Red smiled a little. Biting wouldn't be half as bad as hitting you with a stone. He watched Ruby excitedly. The sharp ecstasy of her vicious temper was beginning to fascinate him.

Ruby was coming back from the car. She had had three swallows of the whiskey, and it felt good to her.

"Well, I'm three up on you." She laughed and her white face was stained with a bright color.

Red went and took the bottle from her hands. Ruby laughed.

"I'm sure goin' around in a whirl. I see you three times. And you don't look so swell three times. You got red hair and freckles big as quarters." Her eyes suddenly darkened and her mouth was drawn in a thin line. "Why'd I ever come out here with you? I hate you." Viciously, she picked up another handful of pebbles.

Red caught her arm, and hit her across the face. She stood as if she were frozen and looked at him. Her eyes were startled. Then she turned from him silently and stumbled back over the sand, and her hair fell before her eyes. She was so disheveled, so young—like a lost child trying to find her way back.

She had disappointed him. Red hated her for that. She had robbed him of his pleasure. She had robbed him of his boast to the men—those older men who had come and gone to small towns all their lives, who had told him how they picked up girls outside hotel windows and gone off in the afternoon. He had picked up Ruby. He had told those men he would show them what a young fellow could do; and they had laughed and made a bet. A swell dinner if he won! But he had lost! And now the swell dinner was on him.

He kicked the sand viciously and every nerve ached in frustration. Then he suddenly thought: he'd show her. Suppose he knocked her down. He'd show her! He'd show her!

He ran down the sand after her, calling her name. The air filled his throat and made him hoarse, but still he called her—still he ran after her.

She stopped when she heard him beside her—and

laughed. It was defiant—deep—and rumbling.

He grabbed her arm. He tried to stop her laughter. He tried to push her to the sand. "Ruby—Ruby—listen to me! I got some swell things for you—silk teddies—and nightgowns with lace—and pink brassieres. I sell them. Don't mean a thing to me to give you a present. I'd like to give you a present."

She was sprawled on the sand. "A silk teddy—a *blue* one with ribbons—I'd like that."

He was down beside her—her face was so beautifully white and so fragile. His hands trembled as he touched her. "Ruby—Ruby—listen to me. Ruby!" He kissed her desperately. "Ruby!"

The kiss angered Ruby. She suddenly hated Red—as she hated Nicki. And the blue satin teddy with the ribbons faded from her mind. She stumbled to her feet and struck him from her.

"Get away from me—I want to go home," she spit at him.

Red swore viciously and followed her to the car.

CHAPTER II

RUBY looked stubbornly ahead of her all the way back to the city. She hardly seemed to know that Red sat beside her. He looked at her furtively trying to understand her strange aloofness. She was different from other girls and he was bewildered. Once he touched her hand, but it was limp and cold to his touch and he quickly drew his own away.

The road was long. The moon was slim and shining like a silver plate in the sky. They followed the curve of the shore. The strains of banjoes and ukuleles came to them. They heard the high pitched voices of amorous singers—broken melodies, sometimes lost entirely in the swishing of the sea. Red studied her face. Her head was outlined against the darkness. Then it came into view as they passed under a yellow road lamp. He drew his breath quickly. Her beauty was different now. Her long hair hung down her neck in a crazy jumble. Her bangs were slashed across her forehead and almost fell into her eyes—her eyes, blue as uncut sapphires and almost as hard.

And still she sat silently—coldly. He was very uncomfortable. It gnawed in his heart that he had been unsuccessful with her, and he wondered what he would say to the men. They would be waiting for him to find out who was to pay for the dinner.

The music came over the water muffled and uneven. Red was miserable. He tried to get her to talk. Ruby's silence frightened him. What was she thinking of? Perhaps she would tell her aunt how he had pushed her down on the sand. Should have known better. Only a kid. His thoughts made his hands tremble once or twice on the wheel. He started to whistle. It was forced: he turned his head to Ruby and tried to be gay.

"How do you like that song they're singing on the water?"

"Pretty good." She didn't even turn her head.

"Lotta people out on the water, singing and making love."

"Yes, lotta people." And Ruby looked like a statue.

Red was thankful for her bits of conversation. He began to feel like his old self again—confident, blustering. Her thin answers made his own gaiety seem less futile. He continued to make conversation.

"Say, I used to like to go out on the water like that—get a canoe—and sing songs. I remember once when I took a girl—Daisy was her name—sure was a beauty—looked somethin' like you—" And a broad smile flashed across his face at the memory.

Ruby turned cold eyes upon him. They struck him like a hammer.

"Why didn't you take me out in a canoe and sing songs?"

He was startled by her remark. She said it in even tones, clear-cut like crystal.

"Why didn't you take me out in a canoe—like that?"

"Oh, I dunno—guess I thought you'd get seasick."

Red laughed foolishly. Then he started to sing.

Ruby touched his arm. "Don't. I just like it quiet —lookin' at the water—and thinkin'—"

Her casual remark stirred an uneasiness in his heart.

"Thinkin'—about what?"

"Lots of things."

"What for instance?"

"My aunt—what she'll say when I get home."

There was a sudden ache in Red's body. His voice was desperate.

"Listen, Ruby—do you tell your aunt every-thing?"

Ruby's voice was cool and husky. "I don't tell her nothin' if I don't want to."

"Then—then you mean—she won't know about me taking you out this afternoon?"

There was contempt in Ruby's answer:

"Don't be afraid. She won't know nothin' about

that. It's school, I mean."

"Oh!"

"She'd wallop the tar out of me for playin' hookey."

Red laughed out loud. It was a harsh laugh broken through in a frenzy from the bottom of his frightened heart. He laughed long and loudly. He touched Ruby's knee with his hand.

"Say, you're a funny kid!"

"You ought to see my aunt when she gets mad sometimes. Takes off her corset and wallops me. Can get cut across the face with that old steel thing she wears."

Ruby lay her head on the back of the seat. She sighed and smiled wearily. Then she closed her eyes. When she opened them again, Red was looking down at her. His eyes were small and brown and warm. She touched his face. It was hot and wet. She drew her hand away quickly. She felt suddenly a great sympathy for this red-headed boy with the frightened heart. She had seen his face turn white when she told him about her aunt and how she beat her with the corset. She had seen him wince and his lip tremble.

"Don't you worry about my aunt, Red. I won't tell her."

She laughed in his face. Her laugh startled him. It was unrestrained and wild. He touched her hand timidly.

"Say, listen, honey—we're almost in town now—just a few blocks and we'll be at the Empire Hotel."

But Ruby didn't stop laughing.

"Listen, kid—I'll drive you to a block from your house—see?"

Then Ruby stopped laughing. Her eyes were suddenly sharp.

"Afraid—eh?"

"No, not afraid—but gee! You know—"

Ruby felt his heart. It was thumping heavily.

"Don't worry. I'll walk home."

The beating of his heart was lighter.

"That's the girl! And maybe I'll see you again tomorrow—huh?"

He looked anxiously toward the electric sign on a bakery. They were already in the city. He drove toward the lights and bore down on the gas.

Ruby jerked his hand. "When you going to give me that teddy?"

He laughed bitterly. "What would I give you a teddy for? For nothin'?"

"You said you sold them—"

"Sure, I do—and sometimes I give 'em away. But not for nothin'. Besides, my stock's at the hotel. Say—you got a nerve!" His face flamed with anger.

She persisted stubbornly, ignoring his fury. "But you told me about the teddy—"

"Listen, baby, you had a chance to get that silk teddy if you wanted it so much—but you turned cold on me! That's a laugh! She wants a teddy!"

"Keep your damn teddy, and keep this, too!" And she hit him across the face again. His nose bled. It stained his tie.

Before Red could stop she had pulled on the brake and was out of the car. He was burning with anger and embarrassment as he wiped the blood away with his handkerchief. There was a sharp pain on the side of his nose. He felt it. It was a cut, a thin sharp cut, and the blood trickled down to his chin. Anger raged within him. He wanted to run her down, to see her yellow hair sprawled in the dirt, to see blood smearing her white face. He wanted to kill her—the damn alley cat! But Ruby was already far down the street.

CHAPTER III

RUBY quietly lifted the latch on the door of the hat shop and went in. It was dark inside, except for the lamp on the table that gave an orange slanting light on the room. She wondered where her aunt was.

Even Nicki, the Greek, hadn't seen her. That was a relief. She didn't want to stop and talk with him, or push him roughly out of her way.

Ruby slipped into a chair underneath the orange light of the lamp. There was a weariness in her eyes as she turned the picture of the bloated ship on the lamp shade from her view. Then she closed her eyes and rubbed her legs.

"So you came home to sleep, did you?"

Ruby looked up. Aunt Carrie, uncorseted, stood in the doorway of her bedroom—an enormous woman. With her hair in tight curls and her body covered with a thin nightgown, she looked grotesquely like some painted animal at a circus. Ruby looked at her with dull eyes.

Aunt Carrie lumbered into the room, and the aroma of lilac came with her—a heavy smell, a futile bid for romance. Aunt Carrie loved the odor of lilacs. She bathed her bulk with scented soaps and dusted it with powders. The blending of the odors of her warm body and the fragrance was overpowering—stifling.

"Did you hear me? Got home all right—didn't you?"

Aunt Carrie lifted Ruby's head. Ruby saw her face with slanting lines from the lamp. And her aunt's lipstick was all down the side of her mouth. Someone must have been kissing Aunt Carrie.

Ruby looked up and saw Nicki standing in the door of the bedroom. She had seen Nicki just that way many times before. His sleek moustache was outlined like patent leather across his fleshy mouth. His curly hair pressed against his head—his face greenish white. She saw him standing there, a sweet smile on his lips—the hateful, saccharine smile that Ruby loathed.

"Nicki here again?"

"Yes, Nicki's here again! And why not? We're going to be married, ain't we?"

And suddenly Aunt Carrie put her hands up to her throat as if to hide her nakedness.

"Yes—when?"

Nicki smiled broadly. Aunt Carrie was outraged.

"Never mind when! What I'd like to know is—where you been?"

"I been out!"

"Sure, you been out! Never got to school, I suppose!"

"I was late."

"Always late!" Carrie took hold of Ruby's shoulder. "Now you tell me where you're been!"

Ruby was defiant. "I was nowhere."

"Don't lie to me, neither! I've tried to make somethin' out of you—tried to do somethin' for you!" She shook Ruby.

"Where you been?"

Ruby turned cold eyes toward her aunt.

"I been out—see?"

"Sure—but where?" She jerked Ruby's head. "Go on, tell me!"

"Leave me alone!"

"You'd better tell me where you been all day— then comin' in like nothin' happened."

Carrie stood over Ruby, puffing with indignation. Ruby regarded with bitterness the enormous woman menacing her.

"Ain't goin' to tell you where I went—none of your damn business!" And she pushed the heavy face away from her. "I went where I liked and I had a good time, see!"

"You did—did you? And doin' what?"

"Doin' what I wanted!"

Ruby got up from under the light of the lamp and walked toward her room. She turned in the doorway.

"I been out with a swell fella—lots sweller than Nicki. And he ain't got a stomach either!"

Nicki's smile faded on his face. He looked at Ruby with dark eyes—dark, brooding eyes. Ruby flung at him viciously:

"Sure, I been out! And had a swell time!" Then she slammed the door.

Carrie turned helplessly to Nicki.

"You hear that, Nick—she's been out—been up to somethin', I bet!"

Carrie's heart was beating violently under the sting of Ruby's defiance. Nicki offered advice. It was given in a muffled tone.

"Sure, Carrie, what you think? A pretty girl like Ruby—"

"The little cat! I'll knock her head in!"

"No, no, Carrie!"

"Yes, I'll give it to her! Been out with some cheap guy. I know it!" Carrie stormed and shook. Her eyes blazed.

"That's it, Nick, she's been up to somethin'." Then her eyes narrowed to slits.

"The damn fool—I bet she never got a thing from him, either."

Nicki lit a cigarette. The flicker of light shone on his hands. They trembled a little.

"You better go ask her again, Carrie. I no like see some smart fella get away so easy."

She hung on Nicki's hand; she whispered hoarsely in his face: "I'll teach her to be easy!"

"What you do, Carrie?"

"I'll get his name—I will! I'll show him! I bet he never gave her a bean!"

Nicki lit another cigarette. There was an evil softness about his smooth, perspiring face.

"Sure, Carrie—you get his name. I get the car. We fix him."

He laughed and touched Carrie's throat with his warm hands.

"Anything you say, Nick. I've tried to make somethin' out of her—ain't I?" Aunt Carrie's heart was beating. "Ain't I, Nick?"

"Sure, sure—you try make somethin' out of her."

He shrugged his shoulders and continued stroking her throat. Carrie smiled and closed her eyes. His hands on her throat were soothing.

"You're swell—you're sure swell, Nick."

Then she opened Ruby's door. Ruby was standing before her mirror, nude.

"Listen, Ruby, I've tried to bring you up to be somethin'. Don't you think I should know who you go around with?"

Ruby hardly heard her aunt. She was looking at her body. It was beautiful. And her face. But was it as beautiful as Red had told her?

Aunt Carrie came closer.

"Listen, honey—tell auntie who he was—the swell guy who took you out."

Ruby shoved her away and sat on the bed. Her aunt sat beside her.

"Bet you had a good time."

Ruby didn't answer.

"Come on, tell me, honey."

Ruby lifted heavy eyes.

"What you want to know for?"

"I love you, don't I? Ain't I brought you up? Tell me what happened."

"Nothin'."

Ruby lay back on the bed and let her legs dangle over the side. Her aunt didn't believe her.

Carrie rose, and started for the door. She sighed. Ruby wasn't going to tell tonight—but she'd get it out of her in the morning.

"Better go right to bed—you got school in the morning."

"I ain't goin' back to school."

"What?"

"You heard me—I ain't goin' back to school."

Carrie broke into hurt sobs. She always sobbed when anyone crossed her.

"Why, Ruby—what's goin' to become of you?"

Ruby was unmoved. She raised her arms over her head, and then quite unexpectedly she laughed. Her aunt looked so funny when she cried. Besides Ruby knew her aunt's tricks. Carrie wanted to touch Ruby's heart so she would tell her about the afternoon on the beach.

"I'll tell you who he was if you want to know so bad."

Aunt Carrie dried her eyes and listened eagerly.

"He's a salesman for silk teddies and nightgowns—sells swell stuff full of lace and ribbons."

Aunt Carrie moaned with delight. "Is that so?"

Ruby yawned. Her eyes closed against her will. Her whole body was fatigued. Aunt Carrie shook her vigorously.

"Go on, tell me—where's he live? What's his name?"

"Empire Hotel. His name's Red—Red Calahan or somethin'."

"And what did he give you?"

"Nothin'."

"He didn't give you a nightie or somethin'?"

Ruby just shook her head.

"Don't tell me that. I know salesmen!"

Aunt Carrie left the room. There was a shrewd look in her eyes as she went to dress and tell Nicki to get the car.

Ruby sat up in bed. It was midnight. Aunt Carrie and Nicki were laughing in a crazy manner. They were singing, too—loud, raucous songs. Ruby put on her kimona and opened the door. Aunt Carrie was draping yards of silk around her. The table was piled high with silk things. Nicki was drinking red wine and rocking back and forth in the chair and watching Carrie. He was singing songs in Greek— strange songs full of melody, and he sang them in his strange tongue. His black eyes looked slumber- ous. He watched Carrie shrewdly, and he drank more wine.

Carrie laughed hilariously as she draped the yards of silk about herself.

"Wait till Ruby sees this—just wait!"

Then she laughed again and ruffled Nicki's hair.

"How do you like me in pink—pink silk, Nicki?"

Nicki smiled and drank more wine. This time he spilled most of it on his shirt.

Ruby watched her aunt. She saw the hideously painted face, looking even more grotesque under the orange light of the lamp.

She walked into the room and touched the flimsy silk things on the table. There were some nightgowns trimmed in lace and ribbons—a green one with pink ribbons—a blue one with yellow ribbons. Some teddies, too. Ruby picked up one of the teddies. It was made of satin and had blue rosebuds on the shoulder. It was the one Red had told her about. She knew because it was so lovely.

Nicki put the wine glass on the table, and his eyes

were feasting on Ruby. He touched her with his hands, and grabbed her to his knee. She tried to get away. But he held her tightly—his soft mouth hot on her face.

"See, Ruby—see what your aunt get for you."

Aunt Carrie held up the bolt of silk.

Nicki rubbed his face against Ruby's. The heat of his face repelled her. She squirmed from his arms and grabbed the bolt of silk from her aunt.

"Did he give you this, too?"

"Sure, he did—didn't have much to fit me—so I made him give me this silk. I can make some nice things for myself."

Nicki waved his glass.

"Sure, Ruby—and he was frightened! We tell him plenty!"

Nicki's laugh was low and musical. "Carrie make him come across. He give nice things for you, too."

Carrie took another glass from the table.

"Come on, Nick, fill her up! Let's drink to Ruby!"

Ruby touched the blue satin teddy on the table, and turned strange eyes on Nicki and her aunt. She said nothing. She suddenly felt sorry for Red. She felt great resentment against these two. They had robbed Red—even though she had persisted nothing had happened. They hadn't believed her.

Her aunt placed a glass of wine in Ruby's hand.

"Drink it, honey—and remember you can always get out of a man what you want!" Carrie was radiant.

"Come on, Nick—sing the funny little song about the cockroach. It's sure got rhythm!"

Nicki sang his songs while Ruby sat on the sofa hugging her blue satin teddy and drinking red wine —watching her aunt drape and undrape herself in the winding bolt of silk she had taken from Red.

Chapter IV

Late the next afternoon, Ruby was shaken out of her stupor. Through heavy eyes she saw Nicki standing over her, calling her name. Nicki was freshly shaved and combed. His velvet face was greenish white through the thick powder, and he smelled of cheap shaving lotion and last night's wine.

"Pretty, Ruby—get up!"

He shook her again. Ruby lifted her head. There was a terrible pain; it went through her like a hammer. Her throat was dry and there was a sickening taste in her mouth.

"What are you doing here? Get out! Where's my aunt?"

She tried to sit up, looking around the room. It was a horrible room in a crazy jumble—empty wine glasses everywhere and a bottle half full of stale wine on the table. The sight of it turned Ruby's stomach. Half burned cigarettes, soggy and bloated, were drowned in the bottom of the glasses—wine-stained and swollen. Nicki had thrown them there.

The blue satin teddy was over her knees. She touched it gently and held it up, and then let it fall lifelessly back into her lap. She closed her eyes again and winced with pain. Her head still ached and she was tired—tired and numb and dizzy.

She felt a hand on her shoulder again. She opened her eyes trying to raise her weary lids.

"Ruby—open your eyes for Nicki!"

He smiled so sweetly. It was a sleek smile and it went from one side of his face to the other—showing one gold tooth in front and even chalk-white teeth on the sides.

"You feel whole lot better when you eat."

The mention of food made her head swim.

"Don't want nothin'."

Nicki's soft hand caressed her neck. She turned her head from his hands, but they would not leave her throat. His voice was soft, too, and thick.

"Poor little Ruby—very tired." And he tried to take her in his arms. She lifted her head suddenly and a terrific pain slit her forehead.

"Where's my aunt? Where'n the hell is my aunt?"

"She get something to eat. Where you think she is?"

He laughed and pushed her hair from her forehead and patted her cheek. Ruby got up, staggered a moment. Nicki caught her to him and the blue satin teddy fell to the floor. Nicki picked it up and wound it around her neck. He ruffled her hair and laughed his low, rumbling laugh. It was a melodious laugh, warm and sweet.

"Make your eyes look more blue."

Ruby fell against the wall. "Take it off, Nicki—take it off!"

"You no like—this nice present?"

"It ain't no present!"

"Sure—betcha your life! Good present, too." And he fingered the silk garment with his soft hands—fingered it appraisingly.

"Beautiful—beautiful—betcha cost five dollars."

"Take it off my neck!"

"Sure—look better on your body. I like see this on you—sometime."

She pushed him away and tore the silk from her neck and threw it on the couch. Only yesterday she had wanted it more than anything in the world. Now it seemed hateful. She stumbled into the kitchen.

The table was half set. Aunt Carrie was stirring something in a pot. It smelled of onions and meat. She held her kimona in one hand and stirred the pot with the other. Her face was without paint—heavy and sodden like cold fat left in a dish. She looked at Ruby and said nothing. Nicki pulled out a chair for Ruby and pushed her up to the table. He walked to the stove and smelled the stuff in the pot. He sniffed in ecstasy.

"Smell good—I like to eat. Maybe Ruby like to eat, too."

"Go on, sit down, Nick."

Carrie brought the pot to the table. She fell into a chair, fanned her face with a newspaper and opened her kimona a little at the throat. She was hot and perspiring, and the flowered thing clung to her body. She puffed and heaved, and last night's curls were limp and thin about her head. They were wet, too, and she pushed them out of her eyes, rolled up the sleeves of her kimona and started to dish out the meal.

"Wonder I don't kill myself—slavin' like I do." And she heaped Nicki's plate full of the stew. It was greasy and thick.

Ruby looked into the pot with dull eyes.

"I don't want no stew." She pushed her plate away. Nicki held it for Carrie to fill.

"Food make you feel whole lot better, baby."

"What's the matter—not good enough for you, I suppose?"

Carrie heaped up her own plate and gave Nicki some extra potatoes. She looked significantly at the plate she had filled for Ruby and Nicki moved it closer to the girl. He was concerned about Ruby.

"I feel sick—I just want some coffee."

"I should think you would feel sick—" and Carrie gave Nicki an understanding look. He smiled a little. Ruby was indifferent as a statue.

"Ain't you got no coffee?"

"Sure, I got coffee."

"All I want is coffee. Where's the pot?"

"On top of the sink. Go make some fresh. Nick wants somethin' to drink after the stew."

Ruby got up from the table, but Nicki caught her hand.

"No—no—Ruby. I make coffee for you."

Carrie peered suspiciously at Nicki.

"What's the idea you bein' so swell to her? Sit down, Nick. She can get it herself—she ain't no cripple!"

"But she a little sick, Carrie."

"I should think she would be!"

Carrie turned cold eyes on Ruby. "Sit down, Nick. I'll get the coffee."

Carrie lumbered over to the sink. Her thick feet made a dull thud on the floor as she dragged herself from the sink to the stove and back to the table.

Her stew on the plate was cold. She fumbled around in the pot and drew forth fatty meat on a bone. Ruby sat quietly. The pain in her head was still sharp. Her back ached. The smell of the meat, buried in the onions, was revolting to her. She looked at Nicki. His plate was clean. His eyes were fastened on her as he leaned back in his chair, and she noticed that the cords in his neck stood out sharp and taut.

Carrie poured the coffee. Nicki drank to Ruby while Carrie put the pot back on the stove. But his voice was very casual as he said:

"Drink, baby—Carrie and I want you should feel better."

The smell of the coffee was good to Ruby. She drank it down in a hurry. Carrie observed her carefully. She was waiting to talk to her. She had many things to say.

"I suppose you know you missed school today?"

Ruby was indifferent.

"What of it?"

"Well, last night was a special night. You ain't goin' on like this—missin' school."

"I told you, I wouldn't go back to school."

Carrie's eyes flamed. A purplish red color spread from her throat to her cheeks.

"I don't know what's goin' to become of you—stayin' out of school."

Carrie began to cry. The tears came quickly and trickled into her mouth. Nicki leaned across the table and wiped her eyes with his hand.

"Don't cry, Carrie—don't cry."

"Did you hear her, Nick? Don't want to go to school—"

"Sure I hear—I hear."

"What's goin' to become of her, Nick? What's goin' to become of her?"

Carrie's acre of bosom rose and fell heavily. The tears continued to gush from her eyes. Nicki patted

her back gently. Ruby looked on defiantly, unmoved.

"What's the good of goin' back—don't learn
nothin'."

Carrie's lips were bloated with tears.

"You're no good—that's what you are—no
good!"

Ruby poured herself another cup of coffee. Her
aunt's tears left her cold. Carrie blew her nose,
trumpeting, and turned elephantine eyes on Ruby.
They were shrewd and bright, and younger than her
face.

"What's goin' to become of you, Ruby? Tell me
that!"

"I don't know."

Carrie sighed explosively, and popped a potato
into her mouth. She gulped a moment and started to
talk again:

"Maybe I wouldn't mind not goin' to school—if
you were willin' to do somethin'."

She gave Ruby a sly look.

"What do you want me to do?"

"Work, of course. Ain't that right, Nick?"

"Well—a pretty girl like Ruby don't need work
too hard, Carrie. I take care of her."

Carrie meant one thing; Nicki meant something
else. He smoothed his hair, gave Ruby an appraising
glance, and spoke in a sweet, gentle voice.

"I know a girl once—pretty like Ruby. She no work too hard—I like her very much."

Carrie opened her mouth wide.

"You don't mean it, Nick?"

"Sure, I mean it. Nicki knows lots of girls."

Carrie frowned. Sometimes she was jealous of Nicki's past. She leaned close until her arm touched his. Nicki was hers—now.

Ruby sat quietly by. The amorous advances of her aunt to Nicki had long ceased to interest her.

"All right, Ruby—if Nick feels that way—you don't need to go back to school."

Ruby didn't answer.

"Did you hear what I said, honey? You don't have to go back to school. Goodness knows you ain't learned much anyway."

Ruby smiled faintly. It was a cold smile, but to Carrie it was a smile.

"You're a fine kid sometimes, Ruby—a real fine kid! Ain't she, Nick?"

"Sure, Carrie—and smart, too."

Ruby's sapphire eyes met the oily black ones of Nicki. He winked quickly and she saw the square gold tooth when he smiled.

Carrie leaned back in her chair and tightened the flowered kimona about her chest guilelessly.

"I forgot to thank you, honey, for the nice pink silk you got me."

Ruby looked startled.

"What pink silk?"

"You ain't forgot so quickly, have you? You earned it all right—me and Nick just went to bring it. Didn't we, Nick?"

The memory of the pink silk and the way they had frightened Red brought laughter to Nick. His eyes swam like black olives in oil.

"Sure—Carrie—sure. You betcha your life— we get it all right!"

"You could get lots of things like that, honey—if you wanted to."

Ruby's face was plaster-white as she regarded her aunt. She saw the loose lip fall away from Carrie's mouth. She saw Carrie's embedded eyes blink as she looked at her.

"Always wantin' to make somethin' out of me— ain't you?"

Carrie caught her breath and turned an innocent face to Ruby.

"Sure, I do, honey."

"No good—that's what you want me to be—no good!"

Carrie's tears cascaded to her kimona. She trembled and shook with sobs.

"I just want you to have nice things—that's what I want. You just ain't got no feelin', Ruby. You're as hard as a rock and me tryin' to do somethin' for you."

Carrie rushed into her bedroom. Her sobs were terrible. Nicki remained in the kitchen with Ruby. She was unconcerned and lovely.

"You're all right, Ruby—I like you."

Nicki leaned across the table.

"What for?"

"Why you say that? I like you because you're so pretty and sweet."

"When you goin' to marry my aunt?"

"Why?"

"I just want to know—that's all."

Nicki pushed the thought aside. "Some night you and me—we go out on the river in a boat. I sing songs—and I tell you—maybe."

Ruby just gave him a contemptuous glance. Her eyes still questioned.

Nicki rose, started toward the door, then he turned:

"Pretty baby, don't worry about Carrie and me. We get married sometime—maybe soon—maybe not." And he was gone.

Ruby leaned back in her chair and closed her eyes. The sight of the cold stew on the table was unpleasant.

CHAPTER V

RUBY never went back to school. She stayed in back of the hat shop, day after day, slopping around in loose, run-down shoes and the blue satin teddy.

She wore that teddy a long time, until the ribbons began to rot and the silk fell apart. But Ruby didn't seem to notice that. She liked the color and the feel of the silk and the way it clung to her body.

"Ain't you ever goin' to take that thing off? I'm tired of lookin' at it." This from Aunt Carrie in a complaining voice.

Ruby looked down at the soiled blue satin. It had completely lost its shining beauty now. It was frayed. A gold safety pin held one of the straps in place. The lace was full of holes. There was lipstick rubbed on the hips. Ruby shrugged her shoulders.

"I like it—"

"But it's gone to pieces. I'd think you'd be sick of it."

Sullenly, Ruby removed the teddy. She kicked it off, then took it up by the strap and threw it under the chair.

Aunt Carrie sat on the unmade bed. The springs collapsed under her weight, and the bed sagged in the middle. She wore her new pink silk, all ruffled and smelling of lilac.

She looked at Ruby's unclad body as the girl lunged across the room, swinging her hips from side to side and humming a tune under her breath.

Carrie pushed her own fat, white-stockinged legs far under the bed as she noticed Ruby's legs. They were white and narrow and covered with a fine gold fuzz.

Carrie sighed again. Her legs had been like that once, long ago. She leaned back against the pillow on the mussy bed; there was a loud creaking again. Ruby turned on her:

"Why don't you get off my bed—makin' noises and bustin' the springs!"

"Wouldn't hurt if you made up this bed once in a while."

"What for? Only to sleep in it again?"

Ruby started to hum the same song.

"Always gettin' up at noon—"

"Why not? I got nothin' to do."

"You could look for a job!"

"I don't want to do nothin'!"

Carrie's face blazed with anger.

"What do you care—eatin' off me—"

Ruby didn't answer. She began humming again. She knew how that irritated her aunt.

"Can't you hum anything else?" Carrie was nervous and angry. Ruby indolently changed her tune. She picked up a pair of step-ins from under a pile of clothes in the closet. Aunt Carrie sat up again on the pillows.

"Guess you think you smell like a violet with them dirty things!"

"They ain't so dirty."

Ruby sprayed toilet water over her body and under her arms. Aunt Carrie watched her closely. She saw her empty the entire bottle of scented stuff on her body. It smelled of violets and was very sweet.

She watched her slip her dress over her shoulders. It was blue and becoming to Ruby. It went with her eyes. It made the blue in them seem brighter, like the blue stones in silver bracelets.

The neck was cut low and wide. The dress was short and swished about her knees. She wore a belt around the waist, and fastened a gold chain necklace about her throat. Then she looked at herself in the mirror. She took a comb and fixed her hair. The bangs fluttered unevenly into her eyes. She pushed them back, then opened a drawer and rummaged through endless ribbons, purses and underwear for a pair of scissors. She started to cut her hair. The bits fell lightly down her throat. Aunt Carrie watched her breathlessly. When Ruby put down the scissors, she groaned with relief.

"You'll go ruinin' yourself yet with them scissors."

"I ain't goin' to cut myself."

"It's your hair I'm worryin' about. Do you want to ruin your looks?"

Ruby surveyed herself in the mirror.

"What's the good of my looks?"

"What's the good of them! All you got—ain't it?"

"Maybe."

"Listen, Ruby—every man likes a good-lookin' girl around."

Ruby was contemptuous.

"How do you know?"

"Well, I know. I've lived a lot longer than you."

Ruby laughed. It was a cruel laugh.

"All men—but Nick—he don't like good looks!"

Her eyes sparkled and she laughed spitefully.

Carrie lumbered over to Ruby.

"Shut your mouth about Nick—see!"

"Sure. I don't want him—he's gettin' fat and his face looks like hot grease to me!"

"You dirty little—!" Carrie picked up the scissors on the dresser and advanced toward Ruby. Her eyes blazed—her hands shook with fury—her thick lips were white.

"Listen here—you better shut your mouth about Nick—see?"

Ruby shrugged her shoulders, and smiled indolently.

"All the same to me!" Then her eyes looked al-

most black as she suddenly grabbed the scissors out
of her aunt's hand.

Carrie whimpered and cowered back against the
wall, trembling. She was breathless and frightened.

"What you goin' to do with them?"

Ruby laughed again.

"Ain't goin' to cut your throat—just my hair,
that's all!"

She cut off two inches from her hair. It hung to
her shoulders—she brushed it all out. It was clear
and fair, and full of yellow lights. She was pleased
with the effect. She tied on her shoes and started for
the door. Aunt Carrie grabbed her arm.

"Where you goin'?"

"Out. Where do you suppose?"

"Out where?"

Ruby snatched her arm away.

"Can't I go out if I want to—without you and
Nick always tryin' to stop me?"

"I ain't tryin' to stop you. I just want to do the
best by you."

"Then leave me alone!"

Ruby pushed her aunt aside and left the room.
Carrie lumbered after her.

"Listen, Ruby—you been out of school two
months now—and you ain't done nothin'."

Ruby was defiant.

"What of it?"

"Well, you got to begin to do somethin'—see?"

"Why?"

"Because my business ain't payin' so well—and I'm gettin' old." Carrie turned on her tears. They gushed from her eyes in torrents. They ran into her powder and streaked her rouge.

"You got no feelin's, Ruby—you don't do nothin' to make me happy."

"What do you want me to do?"

"I don't want you hangin' 'round the house—sleepin' till noon—and then goin' out in the afternoon and doin' nothin'."

Ruby tapped her foot on the floor. Her face looked vicious to Carrie.

"Is that all you want to tell me?"

"Well—don't you think you could do somethin' except always takin' from me?"

"You always got money—you're always buyin' new things for yourself."

"What do you mean? I ain't bought a stitch since God knows when."

"What about the new things I saw in your drawer?"

Carrie's face flushed. Her hands clutched the folds of her dress. Her eyes were burning.

"Nick gave them to me!"

Ruby sneered.

"Catch him givin' somethin' away!"

"Well, he did give them to me—see? He did give them to me!"

"You're a liar!"

Ruby stood against the door. Her body trembled under the blue dress. She could see the furtive look in her aunt's eyes. She saw the mouth dribble in lies. She saw the ugly face, stripped of its paint, fall in heavy sodden lines.

Ruby glanced down on the floor. She didn't want to see that heavy face. But she was thinking of her aunt just the same—wondering. Her Aunt Carrie always had money. Ruby had never bothered to think where she got it. It must have been Nicki. He was making lots of money in his fruit store. Ruby was thinking of other men who had gone before. When they first came to the house they brought candy and fruit and nice things to wear, then suddenly vanished. Maybe Nicki was getting like that.

Ruby regarded her aunt indifferently—and walked to the window and looked out into the alley, thoughtfully. She was untouched by the tears and the loose trembling lips. She had lived with her aunt ever since she could remember. They had always lived in the back of places. They had never had a front door that belonged to a house. Ruby could never remember having a front window that looked out onto the street. They always had back windows that gave on alleys. She knew her aunt had worked for her and brought her up. But Ruby had never loved her.

She remained at the window. She saw a glossy dark cat steal into the alley—a fat cat that walked close to the wall. Ruby was vaguely interested; she felt a similarity in their existence. Then the cat turned its head cautiously from side to side, leaped onto the ash can, and buried its head in the debris. Ruby shuddered.

Carrie's voice came to her:

"You don't care about me—you don't care about nothin' but yourself!"

Ruby's eyes softened.

"All right—I'll go to work. I'll do somethin'."

"A pretty girl like you won't have much trouble."

Carrie wiped her eyes.

"You bet. I'll sell candy—or ties—or somethin'."

Ruby smoothed back her hair and walked through the parlor to the hat shop in front. She opened the door. The bell rang. Carrie ran after her.

"Ruby—Ruby!"

Ruby stopped at the door and put her hands to her hips.

"What do you want now?"

Carrie drew forth an enormous powder puff from the front of her dress. It was covered with fine pink powder.

"Here—wipe it over your face."

Ruby rubbed it over her face. It was cool and smooth. She placed the powder puff on the counter. Her aunt picked it up and held it out to her.

"No, keep it, Ruby—you might need it."

Ruby took it and put it down inside the front of her dress and drew her belt tighter about her waist. She was beautiful. Her aunt smiled at her.

"Gee, Ruby, you sure look like an angel. You got skin like fresh cream—honest!"

Ruby smiled and opened the door again. She swung her hips from side to side and the lace on her teddy showed a little under her dress. She called flippantly over her shoulder to her aunt:

"Ain't I the beauty, though?" She pulled up her stockings and pushed the pink garter farther up on her leg. Her aunt's face flushed for a moment when she saw the pink satin garter.

"You dirty little thief—them's mine! Nick gave them to me!"

The woman grabbed Ruby's leg, trying to pull off the garter. Ruby planted her bright slipper into Carrie's middle and catapulted her against the counter. Carrie fell with a thud, and she looked up, purple with fury.

"I'll tell Nick—see? I'll—I'll—!"

But the bell on the shop door sounded again and Ruby was gone.

Carrie rose clumsily and staggered to the window,

pushing her rumpled bosom in place. She leaned far into the window and watched Ruby walking away from the shop.

Suddenly, Carrie's eyes were young and bright. Ruby would make any man turn around. No girl in this town had hair the color of Ruby's. No one had skin as white as cream and eyes that looked like sapphires. Ruby was sullen and had a temper like a cat. But Ruby was beautiful, too. Her slender face looked like one she had once seen on a picture in a bar room way back in Kansas. It was the picture of a saint, a virgin saint! Carrie scratched her head and leaned farther into the window to catch the last look at Ruby's disappearing figure, and she didn't even notice that she was crushing the crown of her beloved black velvet hat. It would never be the same—that hat!

Chapter VI

RUBY listened to the music in the square. She sat on a long green bench near the pansy bed, and scraped the toes of her shoes in the gravel.

The band was seated high up on a stand, shaded by a huge elm. The band master was elegant, dressed in a shabby red uniform trimmed in gold braid. He waved his baton magnificently, a magic wand, and the tunes he conjured with it were gay and lilting. Ruby was always able to hum them long after she had gone home.

Some Jewish girls went by, wheeling black-eyed babies in carriages. They walked in groups and laughed a great deal. Sometimes Ruby thought the Jewish people must own the park. They took up all the benches. They sat in large groups and told stories. The square was their meeting place. Their lives were arranged in the square. The intimacies of love were whispered from one to the other in the square. The first signs of coming motherhood were excitedly proclaimed in the square.

"Don't look at a black cat—don't lift heavy things—don't be too loving with your husband—and eat good rich food to have a good healthy baby."

All day they sat in the square, wide-bosomed dark girls with soft skins and bulbous high-bridged noses. They wore beautiful clothes trimmed in rich laces and made of fine cloth. They all must have money. Her aunt had once told Ruby that all Jews were rich. Her aunt must be right, for once.

They often looked at Ruby with bold eyes. They were conscious of her white skin and corn-colored hair and her straight nose. But Ruby was indifferent to them. She was filled with music. She never knew that songs could be so beautiful. It didn't matter that she didn't know what they played. Something in her heart pounded when the band master raised his stick and the music came floating down from the stand high up near the tree. Then she would fold her hands on her lap and become very still, alone; alone with tunes, confused and brilliant, beating through her head. It made her think strange things. It frightened her sometimes, when the music rose in a mad frenzy and disappeared in the clouds. She wondered if the violins would splinter in a thousand pieces and burst. She wondered and wondered—and didn't know what she felt and why the music stirred her. She could never explain. She would never tell anyone. There was no one to tell.

Then a tall, dark boy sat down beside her. She had seen him in the square before. She had seen the Jewish girls flutter and blush when he passed. She had seen them flashing their brilliant eyes at him when he walked in the square.

The boy smiled at Ruby, and his manner was easy:

"Hello—all alone?"

"Yes."

"Come to listen to the music?"

"Yes."

"So've I. They've been playing well today, I think —don't you?"

Ruby dug a snub-nosed shoe in the gravel.

"Yes."

"I've seen you before, lots of times."

"I know."

"You always sit on the same bench. I've been watching you and wondering who the girl was that always came to hear the concerts."

He turned heavy lidded dark eyes upon her. Ruby was a little startled. His eyes were the color of Nicki's, but they weren't like Nicki's. They were warm and young and honest. His face was smooth and brown, almost the color of his eyes. Ruby knew he was Jewish. She could tell by his nose. Ruby liked his skin. It was so shining, like polished walnut wood, and his shirt was clean.

"Are you taking piano lessons or violin lessons or singing?"

Ruby smiled.

"No—nothin'."

"But you love music so much. I'm studying the violin—play pretty good, too."

And he leaned forward in the green bench and picked up a handful of pebbles and let them slide through his fingers, and when he lifted his head to Ruby his hair was a jumble over his forehead.

The band started to play "Annie Laurie." It was so plaintive—full of sobbing.

"I like that."

"I knew you would."

"Why?"

"Because you look something like Annie Laurie—yellow hair and blue eyes. You know—'Her brow is like the snowdrift; her throat is like the swan'—"

Something fluttered in Ruby's breast. She put her large dirty hand to her throat, and her face felt warm.

"You're just givin' me compliments. Think I'm a fool—don't you?"

Surprise flushed the boy's face.

"Why, no—I think you're awfully pretty."

Ruby's lower lip curled. She glanced at him disdainfully under her long white lids.

"Men all say the same things to a girl."

"Sure, they do—when they're as pretty as you are!"

Ruby didn't answer. She held her hands in her lap and listened to the last phrases of the song.

"This is the part I like." And she started to hum it under her breath.

High up on the stand, the elegant band master was finishing the song with a flourish.

The music all came together in one magnificent blending, then trembled and blazed forth and suddenly died. The musicians dropped their instruments. The band master bowed and smiled and bowed. The concert was over for the afternoon, but the haunting tones still moaned through the leaves of the large tree.

Ruby sat quietly. The boy listened quietly, too. There was admiration on his face. He ran his hands through his hair nervously and then applauded very loudly.

"That was good. Didn't you like that?"

Ruby nodded her head. The boy still applauded, and there were lights in his dark eyes.

"Sometimes, they play with feeling. Guess they must have played that one just for you! Are you coming here tomorrow?" The boy picked up another handful of pebbles and let them slip through his fingers.

"I don't know."

"Why don't you know?"

"I live with my aunt—and she don't want me to come here."

The boy laughed.

"Oh, I see. You've been playing hookey from school, huh?"

Ruby tossed her head defiantly.

"No, I ain't—I don't go to school!"

"What do you do then?"

"I don't do nothin'."

She sat on the bench like a doll. Her blue dress was up above her knees and the ribbons on her shoes were bright, even though the stubby toes were scarred and streaked with dirt. Her head was shining and fair, and the bangs lay in place across her forehead. The boy looked into her eyes. He lifted her chin with his hand and examined her face carefully.

"My, you're pretty!"

He picked up some pebbles again. For the first time Ruby noticed his hands. They were brown, too, and soft like his face. They were clean and fine, and the nails were short and even. She suddenly saw her own hands. She had never noticed them before. She tried to hide them.

"What's your name?"

"Ruby Wilson."

"Mine's Karl Strassburg. Strassburg Furniture Store—you know."

"That's a big store. I seen a bed there once with a spread I liked. The spread was made of blue silk and ruffled with lace—gold lace."

"Oh, I remember—that was a swell bed. We sold

it to Joe Greenberg for his daughter. She was getting
married."

Then he drew forth a green leather cigarette case
from his pocket and snapped it open. He offered
Ruby a cigarette."

"I don't smoke."

"I didn't think you did."

"I ain't no baby!"

"I know you're not—but I saw your teeth. You
can always tell from a girl's teeth. Yours are ivory-
white."

Ruby started away from the bench. It was getting late. People were beginning to leave the park.
The musicians had gone.

"I gotta go."

Karl caught her hand. She pulled it away quickly
and pushed it behind her back.

"Don't go, Ruby—it's not late."

She stood with her hands hidden from his eyes.

"I gotta go—I gotta look for work today."

Karl ran his fingers through his hair again. It was
a quick nervous gesture. He wanted her to stay.

"But you can't find anything today—it's too late
for that."

"My aunt'll be steamin' like a kettle if I stay here
much longer."

He threw his cigarette away, and stood up beside
her.

"Oh, I see—I know. I'll walk a little way with you, if you like."

The Jewish girls passed Ruby and Karl. They looked suspiciously at Karl. They smiled thin, knowing smiles and looked Ruby over, appraising her and wondering what this pale Christian had that they didn't have.

"Hello, Karl!"

Karl greeted them carelessly. And then they passed on, suppressing smiles.

Ruby stared back at them with cold eyes. She was unaware of the flutter that she sent through their hearts.

"I gotta go—honest."

She walked from him. She looked at her hands again, and closed her fists to hide the broken nails from his eyes. He mustn't see them. He looked so clean and he smelled so nice, and he didn't reek of cheap shaving lotion like Nicki, and his hands weren't hot and oily like Nicki's, either. Karl caught up with her.

"I'll take you home, if you like."

"My aunt don't like men coming to the house."

Ruby didn't know why she said that. But she didn't want Karl to see her aunt. She could picture Carrie peeking through the door of her bedroom and later talking it over with Nicki, and then telling her how much she ought to get from Strassburg's son.

"I'll be here tomorrow—maybe."

"I'll be looking for you, Ruby."

She walked quickly—almost afraid that the boy would follow her. She turned suddenly and he was standing where she had left him, crushing a cigarette under his heel. He waved to her. She waved back and hurried out of the gate. Once more she turned and the boy was gone.

Ruby crossed the street and went past the Empire Hotel. She didn't even look in the window. She hurried past, her head in the air. The tunes of the afternoon were in her ears, and she was swinging her red purse defiantly from side to side.

Chapter VII

SHE thought of Karl all the way home—of his firm brown hands—the pebbles slipping through his fingers. She stopped before a pawn shop, looking into a broken gilt mirror in the window. She held up her hands and saw them in the broken glass. She was glad Karl hadn't seen them.

She crossed the street and stopped before the butcher shop. The butcher was draping strings of sausage on a tray in the window—and Ruby stared at his hands. They were heavy and red. Karl's hands were clean.

She hurried home. There was a customer in the hat shop—Georgia Kaplolski, the Polack's wife. Carrie was fitting a green velvet hat on Georgia's head. Carrie's mouth was full of pins.

Georgia was lumpy and wide, and Ruby saw at once that she was expecting another baby. Maternity was not becoming to Georgia. It distorted her face and thickened her features. It burdened her with weariness—despair. Ruby saw all this in Georgia.

"Gettin' a new hat?"

She indicated the green velvet hat which Aunt Carrie jammed on Georgia's head.

Georgia sighed deeply and crossed her hands over her stomach.

"Yeh—can't get no dresses." She hesitated. "That's the trouble when you marry a Polack—you're always gettin' pregnant."

"A Polack's no different than any other kind," Carrie spoke between her pins.

Georgia sighed again—it was almost a moan. She opened her coat and spread her legs wearily. She was hot and heavy. Her dress was damp and clinging to her body. She fanned her face with a newspaper, and the silk over her large stomach was strained and shining.

"Bill's a good Pole, though, Carrie."

"Sure, you got a good man, Georgia. Bill's a swell guy."

"He sure is, Carrie. He didn't want this kid, though. He thought Violet and Joe was enough for a while."

Ruby was taking it all in. She was always learning something more about men.

"I'm goin' to be smart next time. He ain't goin' to get me drunk no more." Georgia eyed the green hat anxiously. "Say, Carrie—you got to finish that hat before I go to the hospital. I don't want to go there lookin' like the devil."

Ruby was scrutinizing the bloated, freckled face. She remembered Georgia before she was married, four years ago. She was fresh then, and pretty, and her hair had glistened like golden pennies.

"What you thinkin' of, Ruby?" Suddenly Georgia noticed the look of deep abstraction on Ruby's face. "I bet you're thinkin' of some swell guy."

Carrie nodded. "The men are beginnin' to notice Ruby, all right."

"She won't have no trouble gettin' a man with a face like hers. Say, I know a guy'd break his neck for Ruby. He's a friend of Bill—young Pole works in the foundry, and he's strong as a bull."

"Ruby's lookin' higher than a Polack!"

Georgia laughed. She didn't mind Carrie.

"A girl's got to get a good strong man—with lots of hair on his chest to keep the cold away!"

Carrie spit the pins out of her mouth and started to laugh. Georgia broke into raucous laughter, too. Only Ruby felt no laughter—nothing but disgust.

Carrie, still shaking with merriment, pushed the green velvet around on Georgia's head and turned it up on one side. Georgia's pale eyes looked moist and yellow under the hat.

"How do I look, Ruby?" She put her hands on her hips coquettishly. She was like a barrel.

Ruby didn't answer.

"Of course it ain't finished yet—but how do I look, Ruby?"

Ruby bit her lip and her eyes darkened with distaste.

"You look like hell, Georgia—that's what you look like!"

"Well, of all the nasty little cats!" Georgia's face quivered.

But Ruby had disappeared into her room. The sound of their voices followed her. They were talking about her. But all she could think of was—how ugly life seemed.

She threw her red bag on the dresser, beside the morning's coffee, cold and dead in the cup. She looked about the room—such a shabby room. Her clothes were thrown on chairs and were lying about in mussy piles. They made the room stuffy.

She opened the window and pulled up the blind. She breathed in the fresh air. She thought of Karl—his clean hands. Nothing in her room was clean. The sheets on the bed were old and rumpled. She had slept in them for weeks. She pulled them from the bed, and dragged the mattress over to the window.

Then she tore her blue dress off and threw it on the pile of sheets. She kicked off her shoes and stockings. She took off her step-ins and stood before her mirror. Her body looked white. Ruby smiled a slender smile—it looked clean, but it wasn't.

She combed out her hair. It smelled stale, like her skin. She pinned it back on her neck. Again she held up her hands to the mirror. She would scrub them clean—white. She wouldn't hide them behind her back any more. She would hold them out for Karl to see.

Suddenly, the music of the afternoon came back to her. She hummed the tunes. Slowly, she took her kimona off the hook—draped it around her shoulders. She was going to take a bath. She hadn't taken a bath in days.

Chapter VIII

The bath room was a dark narrow room cluttered with things. It had once been a closet. Ruby's old stockings and Carrie's silk underwear, and even ties that belonged to Nicki hung on the towel rack over the tub. A pair of his socks were hanging on a hook back of the door. A blouse of Carrie's, long worn out, dangled over the socks.

A trickle of water was running out of the faucet in the bath tub, and left a yellow stain on the tile. There was a dark rim around the tub. Rusty razor blades were stacked on the ledge. A few had fallen into the tub. Ruby picked them out carefully and started to scrub the bath tub.

She put her kimona over the side of the tub, and then stepped in and turned on the hot water. It covered her toes and part of her leg. It felt good. She lay flat on the bottom of the tub, and laved the water to her thighs and then to her breasts. She lay further under the water, and stretched her legs. The warmth of the water was like a caress. It made her drowsy—languid. Tenderly, she stroked her breasts—she studied them. They were so white—so virginal—smooth as an opal. For the first time in her life, she was beginning to notice her body. She looked into the water at her long thighs—her young legs—her flat slender middle—and a slow throb of ecstasy went through her. Deeper, she slid into the water until it covered her face—and then her head. She closed her eyes.

The water was soft like the touch of his hand—Karl's hand. Ruby smiled. He had never touched her body—but she knew that if he did, it would be as soothing—as gentle as the flow of water over her breasts. Then she lifted her head and her hair clung like wet strands of silk against her face. She patted it down evenly and rubbed it full of soap.

The suds fell in a shower about her shoulders. She laughed like a child and held them up in her hands.

Back in her room, she felt clean and exhilarated. Her hair was fluffy and her skin smelled of soap. She tied her kimona tightly around her and put on a clean pair of stockings.

She stood before the mirror. Her face was clear. Her hair shimmered like fine gold about her head. Then she saw Nicki sneaking across the alley—like an evil tom cat. He waved his hand and threw her a kiss. As he came to the window he leaned on her mattress.

"Hello, Ruby. What you do today? Wash your pretty hair?"

"None of your business!"

She tried to pull the mattress from the window.
Nicki laughed at her efforts, bearing heavily on it.

"You damn Greek! Get away from my mattress!"

Ruby spoke through her teeth, and her lips were
white. But Nicki was calm and smiling.

"Sure—I no want your mattress."

"Then get away!"

Nicki put his hand through the open window and
pulled her kimona from her shoulders.

"Beautiful Ruby."

"Leave me alone!"

Her eyes were dark with hate. Nicki's voice was
soft.

"I like see you so pretty and so mad—like a little
kitten."

And he pushed his hand under the window pane,
trying to touch her skin—to tear her robe from her
—to see her nude.

She pulled out the stick that held up the window.
It fell with a thud on Nicki's wrist. His face contorted with pain, and he swore viciously. Ruby's
eyes danced madly as he dragged out his hand. It
hung limply. He shook it, but it still hung limp at
his wrist. His face was not smiling now. His black
eyes were like flaming coals.

"Now will you leave me alone!"

He shook his wounded hand.

"Sure—I leave you alone!"

Then, nimbly, he slipped through the window and caught her to him.

"Leave me alone, Nick!"

"Sure, Ruby, sure. I just want show you my hand. Look what you do to Nicki!"

He held out the bruised hand to her. There was a welt across the back. She looked at him defiantly.

"Serves you right! I ain't goin' to let you touch my mattress with your dirty hands!"

"No, I like better touch you pretty body with hands."

His voice was purring. She felt his arms damp and hot around her. Nicki laughed and pushed her head back. He tried to reach her lips.

She struggled to loosen his arms, but they clung to her. They were strong as iron—ape-like arms.

"Why you no like me, Ruby?"

He kissed her throat. It quivered under the touch of his lips. She snarled through her teeth:

"Get out of my room!"

But he only laughed melodiously.

"You very pretty, Ruby."

She twisted in his arms.

"I'll tell my aunt!"

Nicki's eyes darkened, but only for a moment. He held her so tightly against him that she couldn't breathe. She felt hot and stifled and crazy. She wanted to hit him across his gold teeth. Tears came to her eyes. Tears of fury and disgust. She felt so helpless and it angered her.

He laughed again and then he kissed her ravenously. Ruby stiffened in his arms. She closed her lips firmly.

"Why you no like Nicki?"

"My aunt—I'll tell her."

Viciously, Nicki tore the kimona from her and crushed the words on Ruby's mouth. Then he buried his teeth in her throat. The pain stabbed her.

"Damn you! Damn you!" She fought like a cat.

He held her still. He liked the taste of her flesh.

Suddenly, she wrenched herself away—covered herself with her kimona. She picked up a vase from the table.

"I'll kill you if you touch me again!"

She threw the vase at him. It crashed to the floor as Carrie opened the door.

There was a moment of tense silence. Then Nicki held out his wounded hand to Carrie.

"What happened, Nick—tell me?"

Coldly Ruby explained:

"I jammed the window on his hand, and I broke the vase. Nick and me were havin' a fight."

She turned on her heel and left the room. As she slammed the door, she flung back at them:

"Tell her about it, Nick."

Nicki smiled a sickly smile.

"Nice, sweet, little kid—this Ruby."

Carrie started to pick up the broken pieces of the vase.

"Well—she got a rotten temper. Say, listen to me, Nick, if I thought she threw this vase at you I'd kill her—honest to God!"

"No, Carrie, no!"

"Gee, Nick, if anything happened to you—I'd die—honest I would."

Carrie's voice faltered and broke. She rubbed her jowls on his chest and closed her eyes. He closed his eyes, too. She liked the smell of his shaving lotion, and she liked his thin silk shirt that clung to his back. There was little of her *he* liked.

"Come on, Nick—I got somethin' good for you. I bet you ain't had a thing to eat."

"You pretty good to me, Carrie." He forced himself to say this, and to kiss her poppy-colored cheeks. She clung to him.

"Sure—you're pretty good to me, too, Nick."

Carrie was glad that Ruby was not there.

CHAPTER IX

RUBY went to the Square every day to meet Karl Strassburg and hear the concerts. Sometimes Karl was late, but Ruby knew he would come.

He never went directly to her bench. She used to see him walk quickly through the entrance of the park and then stroll leisurely from bench to bench, talking to his friends, or throwing pebbles in the fountain, or smoking cigarettes abstractedly as he leaned near a tree listening to the chatter of one of the Jewish girls.

Then he would look up suddenly and smile at Ruby—a faint smile but full of meaning. He always greeted her eagerly as though he had come upon her by surprise. But she knew he had come to the park only to see her. Then as he slid into the seat beside her, his voice was casual:

"Hello, Ruby—how are you today?"

He pulled a limp cigarette from his pocket.

"I had a tough time getting away from the store—my father wanted me to go down to the factory. He always has something for me to do when I want to get away."

"I know—my aunt's the same."

"Didn't try to keep you away today, did she?"

"Well, I came anyway."

"I'm glad."

"She thinks I'm lookin' for a job."

"She doesn't like music—your aunt?"

"Sure—when it comes out of a phonograph and plays something from a dance."

"She's not much like you—is she?"

"No—she ain't like me. She ain't nothin' at all like me!"

"Nobody could be just like you, Ruby."

Karl looked tenderly at the pale face beside him—at the eyes grown sullen.

"You're beautiful, Ruby, and you don't know it. And you've got something—I knew it the first time I saw you."

Karl's face was young and eager and sincere. He spoke honestly. His eyes were brooding—tense. Ruby laughed quietly.

"Sure—I know—I got big hands—that's what."

Karl took up one of her large hands and held it in his own. They were always clean now.

"They're artistic hands—long and narrow."

"Who told you?"

"I've read it in books. Besides I know how you like music. You got a voice, too, Ruby."

"You got music—that's what you got, Karl. Maybe some day you'll be playin' in a band like that."

Karl sighed and drew his hand through his hair.

"I'd like to—but my mother wouldn't let me. She wants me to stay in the furniture store. We got a big business, you know."

"I wish I could play the violin, or sing, or somethin'." There were dreams in Ruby's eyes.

"Why don't you take lessons, Ruby? Start in now."

"I ain't got money—and my aunt don't like the kind of music that costs somethin'."

"She wants you to work?"

"Sure—that's what my aunt wants."

Karl laughed happily.

"What would she say if she knew you were meeting me here every day?"

Ruby looked ahead of her and clenched her hands.

But the bitterness in her eyes vanished when she heard the first bars of the Spring Song.

The band master had raised his baton. The music had begun.

"Listen—listen! It's goin' to be swell!"

Karl edged very close to her and took her hand. He only half listened to the music when she was so close to him. He was fascinated by her hair. He liked to watch the sun caress it—become tangled in it. He liked to watch her hands fumble nervously in her lap when the music pleased her. He liked to watch her eyes as the violins played and the tones poured down from the tree, clear and rich. He saw the dark blue of them flicker sometimes, and then they seemed far away, and almost black.

He leaned back against the bench and watched her quietly. She smiled at him—and he held her hand tightly until the concert was over.

She was always so filled with the music she hardly noticed how he dropped her hand quickly as though he were embarrassed, when some of his friends passed the bench. He nodded to the Jewish girls and pushed his hands deep into his pockets. He pretended not to see their wise looks and smug smiles when they spoke to him.

"Hello, Karl—how did you like the music?"

"Great! Good concert today."

His tone was casual, but they saw through it and their laughter chilled him as they walked away and glanced back at Ruby. He looked after them furious. And when they were out of sight he caught Ruby's hand again and held it tightly.

"Guess they want to know all about you, Ruby."

"Those girls?"

"You bet. They've seen me sitting here with you every day for two weeks."

"Do you care, Karl?" There was something strange in her face.

"Care? About what?"

"About me—sittin' here every day—like this?"

"Of course not. What do I care what they think. Does it worry you?"

Ruby didn't answer for a moment.

"Does it?"

She hesitated, then stumbled on the words.

"Yes—Karl."

He was startled. He had never realized that the looks of his smug friends had hurt her.

"Why, Ruby—what do you care what they think?"

She took her hand away from him and let it lie in her lap. Then she grabbed the handle of her purse, and nervously clasped and unclasped the lock. She said very softly:

"Because you're a Jew, Karl—and I ain't— that's why. I know what they're thinkin'."

He picked up a handful of pebbles and threw them one by one against a tree, aimlessly. He didn't look at Ruby, but she looked at him and she saw that his mouth was set, and there were lines between his eyes. His face looked suddenly thin. He seemed nervous.

"That doesn't make any difference, Ruby. They always think things like that when a Jewish fellow in this town starts going around with a pretty Christian girl."

"I know." Her face was sullen and bitter. "Don't

let's talk about it—after the music."

Ruby loved coming to the park like this, and meeting Karl. She loved to get up in the morning feeling fresh, like the sun, and think she was going to see him that afternoon. She liked to stand naked before her mirror and look at her body, now so white and clean and smelling of fresh soap.

Both Carrie and Nicki could see that Ruby was different, and spying upon her, they wondered. But they couldn't understand—they could only wonder. Ruby lived alone in her room and the blind was pulled down on her window.

Nicki could never see her when he passed through the alley to her aunt's room. She had seen Nicki many times since their fight. He always looked at her with a thin smile on his face. And she could feel his eyes fastened on her back when she turned from him, but Ruby kept out of his way. She passed her aunt, too, with indifferent glances and slipped through the shop door to go to the park. Her aunt used to watch her go, and wink at Nicki. But Ruby didn't mind that. She was thinking of meeting Karl, and the songs were already starting to play in her head. And then she wished that Karl hadn't been Jewish.

So they sat on the bench together. And when the concert was over and she touched his arm, she always said the same thing.

She said the same words today:

"I gotta go."

He always delayed the parting moment:

"No, no. I want to talk to you, Ruby. I hate to leave you after these concerts. Ruby—Ruby—you're like the music to me."

"Am I?"

"I could get my father's car some night and we could ride out somewhere—some place where we'd be alone."

He pushed her bangs from her forehead gently—so gently that Ruby wanted to cry. But she bit her lips and her throat filled. She was embarrassed. She didn't want Karl to think she was a fool. Anyway, she couldn't explain to him why she wanted to cry. She couldn't explain that he brought the tears because he spoke so low and he touched her head like it was made of china and afraid it would break.

"You're a doll, Ruby—a great big lovely doll! Will you go with me—will you?"

"When you want me to go?"

"Tonight—I'll get the car. I'll tell my father I need it." His dark skin was flushed and his eyes were eager and fierce and he held her hand warmly in his own.

"I'll meet you on the corner—at Maple street. You know—by that big statue. Wear that blue dress of yours." He tilted her chin and laughed in her eyes.

But her face was solemn and pale.

"I hate that blue dress—makes me look like hell!"

"No, it doesn't." He was sincere. "It makes you look pale like a china doll—that's how I like you to look."

"A swell china doll I'd make!" she laughed.

"I never saw a girl with a face like yours."

Ruby looked at Karl under her lids. Her eyes seemed almost black. She was happy.

"Honest?"

"Honest, Ruby." He looked at her tenderly. She sat very still.

The people who passed by their bench never suspected the happiness in her sapphire eyes. They only saw a lean dark Jew and a blond girl with shapely legs, sitting together on a bench, and the girl was fumbling with her skirt, and the skirt was short and green.

Chapter X

THEY had been driving for a long time. Ruby hadn't said a word. Karl tightened his arm about her shoulder.

"Are you thinking of me, Ruby?"

She didn't answer. She was afraid to tell him that she had been thinking of him all the way. She was ashamed that he should guess her thoughts.

"I dunno—what I'm thinkin' of." Her face was impassive, but her throat was parched.

"Let's park awhile—I want to talk to you."

He stopped the car under the bridge and they both watched the water gush over the rocks and break into foam—and quite unexpectedly he took her in his arms and kissed her wind-swept face.

"I sure like you, Ruby."

"Do you?" her voice was husky.

"I keep thinking of you all the time—ever since that day I saw you in the Square."

He took her hand and rubbed it vigorously between his own.

"You're so pretty"—he hesitated—"no, not just pretty. That isn't the word. *White*—white as milk. And your hair is so blond. I don't know—I just can't stop thinking of you—that's all!"

Ruby sighed. It was a happy little sigh.

"I bet a lot of fellows told you that before."

She looked at him intently a moment.

"Sure."

She was thinking of that afternoon on the beach —of Red and their ride together. He had told her something like this. Karl told her quietly what Red had said through thick soft lips. But it was the same —just the same.

She pushed his arm away and opened her purse and took out a powder puff and daubed it over her face.

"Sure, I'm a swell girl, I am." And she licked her tongue over her lips, wiping off the fine sweet powder.

"Ain't we goin' somewhere?"

"Where do you want to go?"

"Any place."

"Let's drive out to Jersey Point—it's not far."

But he didn't start the car. They sat together silently watching the dark water under the bridge.

"Did you have a tough time gettin' the car?"

Her deep voice broke the silence.

"In a way."

"Bet your father wanted to know where you was goin'?"

"I told him—he doesn't mind—didn't need the

car."

"Bet your father didn't know I'm a Gentile."

"I don't know what he knows. It doesn't matter anyway."

"Ain't mad—are you?"

"No, of course not, Ruby."

"I thought you was. I—"

He jerked her head back and looked into her face.

"I'm mad about you, Ruby." He was tense as he kissed her and held her firm against his chest.

"Don't you like me, Ruby? Tell me!"

She could hardly hear his voice. It was almost a whisper—and thick.

"I like you."

"But I don't mean like that. I mean—don't you understand how—how I feel? Don't you?"

He couldn't say any more. Suddenly he buried his head in her lap, and his dark hair fell in a jumble. She sat quietly, afraid to move. She wanted to touch his head and lift it. She wanted to tell him so many things she felt—but she couldn't. She was all mixed up and her emotions left her inarticulate.

"Karl—you're—you're swell!"

She stroked his hair with an awkward hand. Her fingers fumbled in his dark head. She was trying to express what was deep in her heart.

"You make me feel—like—the music makes me feel."

He lifted his head. Their eyes met.

"You got nice eyes, Karl."

He caressed her straight, fair hair.

"I can't take you back home—tonight."

"Why?"

"You're a funny girl—don't believe me when I say I'm mad about you."

"I believe you."

"Then let's not go home."

"I'm cold—honest."

"We'll drive down to my father's factory. It's warm there."

"I never been in a factory."

"There'll be nobody there—but you and me," he said eagerly.

"I better go home, Karl."

"No—no, Ruby—not tonight. Don't you want something to eat first—hot chocolate or something?"

She wet her lips with her tongue.

"Hot chocolate—I'd like that."

He started the car. They passed houses and stores and other cars. Then they stopped outside a little restaurant, far back from the road.

"Here we are!"

She looked around. They were quite a distance from town. She knew that. This was Jersey Point— Karl's father's factory was not far. They got out of the car. He pulled her over under a light. She was beautiful—and her wide mouth looked as if it had been lacquered red and her lips were damp.

"You'll do, Ruby—any time for me!"

He took her arm and they walked toward the restaurant. It was almost twelve. Ruby drew in her under lip and thought of the unpleasant fury of her aunt when she got home. But as they went into the place, the smell of coffee and fried eggs made her forget everything except that she was hungry.

"What do you want, Ruby?" They climbed up on the high stools and leaned on the counter.

"Fried eggs and coffee and plenty of ketchup!"

"The same for me!"

The eggs broke and sizzled on the pan. Ruby watched them and inhaled the smell.

"I sure had a good time tonight, Karl."

"Did you?"

"Sure."

"That's great. We'll do this often. My father's factory is only a little ways from here."

"I know it."

"Let's go there."

"My aunt'll kill me if I stay out any later. She's givin' a party tonight."

"Then she won't miss you."

"You don't know my aunt. I gotta go, Karl."

The restaurant keeper placed the fried eggs in

front of her. They were golden brown in thick grease. Ruby was hungry.

"This is a swell place!"

The restaurant keeper smiled understandingly and put a doughnut on her saucer when he gave her the coffee. She bit in it and licked the jelly quickly. Karl watched her. Suddenly, with the jelly on her mouth, she seemed such a kid to him. Perhaps she'd never gone out before with a boy—a Jewish boy who wanted her more than anything else.

They didn't go to his father's factory that night.

CHAPTER XI

CARRIE was entertaining company when Ruby got home. It was a gay party. The table was piled high with sandwiches and empty gin bottles. Georgia was on the couch nibbling an apple. She greeted Ruby with a smile. Her approaching maternity made it difficult for her to get up and greet Ruby as she would like to do. Georgia's husband was leaning against the piano drinking sulkily out of a tall glass. Her condition had soured him. He regarded Georgia with dark resentment. Her tawny hair that once maddened his senses was a matted lusterless mass on the cushion, its brilliant redness gone. He smiled when he saw Ruby. She was slim and young and her abdomen was flat. He set the glass on the piano and pulled her to him.

"How are you, Ruby?" His voice was thick like his face. She drew back.

"What's it to you?"

Her gesture brought back his sulkiness.

"Don't see you no more. Why don't you come see Georgia—sometime?"

Georgia raised her head at the mention of her name, like an indolent walrus.

"What's he sayin' to you, Ruby?" There was the sickly whine of the pampered convalescent which she arrogated to herself—only because she was not that to Bill. Bill interrupted sharply:

"I tellin' her lots of things!"

Georgia laughed bitterly.

"I bet you are—you're such a great guy, you are!"

She fell back on the pillow. Bill's face flushed with fury. He picked up his warm drink and shrugged his thin shoulders.

"I be glad when you get baby—you look just like a cow!"

He laughed harshly, cruelly, and Georgia burst into tears. Carrie ran to her, while Ruby looked on.

"Don't mind him, Georgia—he's drunk, that's all!"

Carrie turned on Bill.

"You're a big slob, Bill, to make her cry when she's expectin' any minute." She patted Georgia and offered her a glass of wine. Georgia lifted her bloated face from the pillow and sipped it. Carrie brightened again.

"Come on, somebody—this ain't no funeral. Put on some more music and let's dance."

She put an arm around Ruby.

"I got a surprise for you—a swell guy. He's in my room playin' cards with Nick on the bed."

"I don't want to meet no one."

Carrie was hurt.

"You gotta be polite—ain't you? I promised I'd bring you in."

"I don't want to meet him."

"Elegant, ain't you—and just because you been out with a rich Jew!"

"What of it?" Ruby was defiant.

"You think you're swell—that's what you think! Cheap one, he is—never gave you nothin' to bring home—not even a pair of garters!" Carrie laughed shrilly. "You pick a Jew what's got somethin' and you ain't even got sense enough to get it!" Carrie hulked squarely before her.

Ruby's eyes narrowed in a thin, hard line. She pushed her aunt out of the way.

"I'm goin' to bed!"

Carrie caught her arm.

"Don't go yet, honey," shrewdly. "You might be sociable. Say somethin' to Joe. He's been askin' for you all evenin'."

"I got nothin' to say to him." She was thinking of Karl—and the long ride in the wind—and the feel of the cold air on her cheeks.

The strains of the victrola came from the parlor. Bill had put on a dance tune. Ruby listened for a moment. The song was full of melody. She smiled faintly and hummed it under her breath. Carrie continued to urge her:

"Joe'll love to dance with you."

Ruby didn't answer.

Nicki opened the door from Carrie's room. He was holding some cards in his hands. His pink silk shirt clung to his damp skin. He smiled when he saw Ruby.

"Hello, Ruby. Where you been so late? I wait for you—sure—me and Carrie!"

He threw the cards on a table. Ruby noticed that the palms of his hands were damp, too.

"Pretty hot in your room, Carrie. You got too much perfume and too much petticoats, everywhere!" And he laughed and showed his gold tooth. He turned to the room again:

"Come out, Joe. Don't fix up too much for Ruby. You look good."

He put an arm around Carrie's thick waist.

"I win thirteen dollars from Joe. He don't like that!"

Carrie laughed. "Come on, Nick—we gotta dance to that swell music." She was anxious to feel his embrace if only in a dance. But Nicki had eyes for Ruby alone.

"No, we wait for Joe. I promise him Ruby dance with him." He turned to Ruby: "What you say, little baby?"

"You got a nerve, you have! I ain't dancin' with no one. I'm goin' to bed!"

Nicki called off to the bedroom:

"You hear that, Joe? Don't put on no more perfume. Ruby go to bed!"

Joe entered. Ruby looked at him sullenly. He was tall and powerful, with straight blond pompadoured hair that stood up like fine wires. His face was leather brown, and his eyes pale blue.

Nicki leaned against the door and watched Ruby. His jaw tightened when she lifted her head and shook her yellow hair out of her eyes.

"This is Joe, Baby. He want dance with you."

Joe smiled and showed his square uneven teeth. But the music had stopped.

"Hey, what's the matter? Come on, we want more music!"

"Sure, we do, Nick—you're right!" Carrie was swaying on her thick ankles and snapping her fingers to the tempo of the dance record. "Come on, let her go!" Carrie stood waiting for Nicki's arm, but he turned from her and pulled Ruby into the parlor.

Georgia, on the sofa, was heaving and tossing heavily while Bill danced with a thin girl in a tight yellow dress. He hardly looked at Georgia. His face was buried in the girl's hair. It was fuzzy hair, and almost white, and looked like wool. Ruby hadn't noticed her before.

Carrie interrupted Ruby's glance. "That's Hazel —thought she wasn't comin'." Then to Hazel:

"How'd you come to take a night off? Ain't business good?"

"Sure, it's good. But I gotta take a night off sometime. It's an awful strain runnin' that place—keepin' the girls in good humor." And Hazel sighed.

She didn't raise her head. She was engrossed in Bill, concerned with his surreptitious pawing.

Carrie's eyes riveted on Nicki and Ruby dancing together.

"Can you beat that?" she winced. Then she heard Nicki's voice. He was singing to Ruby and the tone was rich and low. Carrie leaned against the piano and fanned her quivering heart with a sheet of music. Nicki's voice always made her heart quiver. She had known him now for three years, and clung to him desperately; had tried in every way to bind him to her, to make herself necessary to his happiness—to his comfort. She smiled to herself. She was necessary to his comfort. Hadn't he told her so? And now he had danced off with Ruby.

There were tears in Carrie's eyes, tears of humiliation. She walked over to the sprawling Georgia.

"How you feel, Georgia?"

Georgia tossed wearily.

"Lousy—I want to go home."

Carrie patted her shoulder. "Go on, you look swell. Ain't had no pains yet—have you?"

But Georgia's travail had begun.

"Where's Bill?" A spasm passed over her face. "I—I wanta go home!"

Carrie couldn't tell her that she had seen him go into the hall with Hazel carrying two bottles of liquor. She looked down at Georgia's feverish face.

"I'll find him, Georgia."

Carrie pushed Georgia's matted mop from her forehead and gave her a drink of water.

"How do you feel now?"

Georgia smiled weakly.

"Not—not so—good."

"I'll go get Bill."

Carrie found Bill and Hazel on her bed. They didn't see her. She closed the door hastily.

"My God—and this is Hazel's night off," she breathed to herself.

Carrie didn't know what to tell Georgia. She started toward her—but Joe suddenly put his arm about her. He was holding her close.

"I wanta dance this hot number with you, Carrie!"

She blushed.

"Aw, go on—do you, Joe?" Her eyes arched coquettishly; her brashly crimsoned mouth puckered. He wondered what Nicki saw in her.

"Sure, I do. We can't let this music go to waste!" And he swung her roughly out on the floor. With elephantine coyness, Carrie nestled close to him. She liked his rough manner and she quite forgot about Georgia and Bill. Nicki's voice came over Joe's head. But this time she didn't even listen. Her pride was no longer hurt. She was just as good as Ruby—dancing with a younger man than Nicki—and he was as strong as a bull.

Nicki danced by. "She's pretty good, eh, Joe?"

Joe winked at Nicki and swung Carrie around furiously.

"Hey, not so fast—what you think Carrie is?"

Joe laughed and pushed Nicki off the floor. He fell against the table, Ruby on him. He clung to her.

"Don't go away from me, Ruby." His dark eyes mellowed and shone. "I wait for you all night, baby." And he pulled her closer to him.

"Leave me alone. Dance with my aunt—that big Polack'll kill her!"

Nicki laughed.

"Nobody kill Carrie. She strong like big horse. I know her! But I like to know you, Ruby. You so mad all the time—so much like fight. You no like me, I suppose?"

He brushed her throat with his damp hand. She drew her head out of his reach. Her lips were drawn tightly. She almost spoke through her teeth:

"I hate you—sweaty Greek!"

Her words cut him. He wanted to crush her—to beat her—to feel her fluttering hair against his face.

But he spoke to her softly—gently:

"You don't think that, sometime—when I sing for you. I watch your face—your eyes. They are happy. You like Nicki when he sings."

"Maybe."

"Then I sing for you now. I sing anything you like—Italiano—Caruso—Pagliacci—anything!"

"Leave me alone!"

She jerked away from him and dodged into her room. He looked after her bitterly and his eyes were streaked with blood.

The music had stopped. Carrie and Joe came to him. Carrie was puffing and smiling.

"Gee, it was swell. Nick could never've danced like that!"

But Nicki didn't hear her.

"What's the matter, Nick? Don't you feel well?"

"I feel good, Carrie."

Joe put another record on the victrola.

"Where's my girl—Ruby?"

Nicki caught at his arm. "She go to bed, Joe— better dance with someone else!"

Nicki's skin was lifeless and green. Joe laughed good-naturedly:

"Carrie picked her out for me!"

Carrie watched Nicki a moment. He turned his eyes from her. He couldn't abide her painted face. The feel of Ruby's golden hair was still on his cheek.

The line of her throat was still seared into the fibre of his brain. The defiant, vicious look of her still consumed him.

"We better go get a good drink, Joe." He tried to be casual.

"I don't want no drink. I came here to dance with Ruby—and I'm going to dance with her!" Joe was obstinate now, and sullen. His blue eyes were veneered in granite. Carrie stood by, watching them with interest. She liked a fight. Nicki's face relaxed in a smile.

"Sure, I go call her, Joe. I tell her that!"

Carrie's face flushed.

"You ain't goin' to do nothin' of the sort! This is my party. We got other people here beside you, and Ruby, and this big Polack. You got to be sociable, Nick." She took his hand.

"Come on, I want you to meet Hazel."

It suddenly came to Carrie that Bill and Hazel— she had forgotten them. And she must get him away from her. Then she thought of Georgia.

Georgia was in the parlor, pain-wracked—a contorted mass on the sofa. Her hands clutched her dress frantically. Her head rolled from side to side, a doleful moan came from her parched lips.

"Bill—Bill!" She tried to raise her head. With an effort she sat up, leaning on her elbow and breathing heavily. "Bill—Bill!" The perspiration stood out on her forehead. She clutched her stomach as a spasm of pain went through her. She whimpered: "Bill!" Then a shriek escaped from her swollen lips. "Bill!" She was sobbing now bitterly, unrestrainedly. She was bewildered with pain, and alone, and became suddenly frightened.

"Bill! Bill!" She cried out in anguish, and rocked back and forth on the couch.

The door opened. He was looking at her, his hair mussed, his face pale.

"I gotta go, Bill—it's here!"

She looked helpless and messy. His jaw tightened. He went to her, and put his arm about her. She leaned against him, and he turned his head away. Her agony was repulsive to him.

"Carrie!" he called harshly.

Carrie rushed into the room.

"You go get Nick's car. It's comin'!"

Carrie, frightened, began to tremble. Her eyes bulged.

"Nick's had an argument with Joe. He's mad as the devil. You ask him, Bill."

Another shriek from Georgia.

"Georgia's got pains, Carrie! She got to go to the hospital!"

"Sure, I know, Bill. Gee, the poor kid! Bet it feels like hell." Carrie wrung her hands desperately. "Sure, I'll get Nick—I'll go to the hospital, too.

Poor kid!"

Bill put an arm under Georgia's limp body. She held his free hand until the nails cut into his flesh. Dull moans came from her closed lips.

"I feel like hell, Bill. Shouldn'ta come tonight!"

"Sure, I know—always like that!" reproachfully. She had indeed spoiled it for him.

She looked at him in anguish.

"You ain't sore—are you?"

"No, what for I'm sore! Only hard luck"—the last to himself.

"I dunno—because—because you were havin' such a swell time—and—and—"

Georgia couldn't finish. Bill smiled a thin, twisted smile. He was thinking of Hazel and her hair like wool; she was waiting for him in Carrie's room.

Georgia tried to lift her head. "Gee—where's Nick?" She cried out again: "Where's Nick—the car! Bill—do somethin'—will you?" Her voice cut like a knife. "I'm goin' to die with this pain!" The veins stood out on her forehead.

Carrie returned with Nicki. The Greek was excited. Georgia's feverish face stirred him.

"Sure. I get the car right away—sure!"

Georgia smiled at him pathetically and tried to get off the couch.

"I can't walk, Bill—I'm crippled!" And she fell against him.

He cradled her bulk in his arms. Her face was white and lifeless. Her new green velvet hat fell on the floor, forgotten.

Carrie grabbed a bottle of wine from the table:

"Hurry up. Gee, poor kid! The poor kid!"

Bill saw Hazel standing in the bedroom doorway. She looked at him with a strange smirk. She leaned against the door and watched him stumbling down the stairs with Georgia—and Georgia's hair hung crazily over his arm. Carrie and Nicki followed.

Joe and Hazel were left alone. He looked at her awkwardly.

"Funny party tonight—lots of excitement."

She nodded, and ran her brightly colored bracelets up her arm.

"She would have pains just as we were havin' a good time. Say—I'm starved."

"I know a good place to eat—and dance, too."

Hazel shook her head.

"Yeah?"

"Sure! We can't go home, early like this—because somebody is havin' a baby."

Hazel was defiant.

"I thought you were fighting with the Greek because you wanted to dance with Ruby."

Joe laughed heartily—to cover up the hurt to his pride.

"No—I don't want her."

Her lips curled disdainfully.

"She went to bed alone—left you. You must be a great guy!"

"Sure, I'm a great guy—pretty strong! Let's go somewhere, and I show you!"

Hazel flashed him a smile. If it was meant to tantalize him, it did. Then she put on her hat.

"A swell party this is. Say, you don't catch me gettin' married!"

Joe nudged her roughly and he felt her skin, soft under her tight yellow dress.

"Come on, Baby—you and I goin' to have good time."

She shook her jangling bracelets.

"Okay, mister—I'm feeling good." Then suddenly:

"Look, she forgot her hat."

Hazel laughed and picked up Georgia's green velvet from the floor and put it on the table.

"Poor kid—I felt sorry for her. She sure got some husband, though!"

Joe grabbed her arm. The tinkling bell on the hat shop door sounded as they stepped out on the street.

Hazel drew a deep breath.

"Gee! I ain't had a night off in God knows when!"

"Yeh! A trolley car givin' a motorman a ride."

Hazel's thin laugh echoed on the night.

"You got it all balled up, mister!"

Chapter XII

Ruby hadn't seen Karl for over a week. The Strassburg Furniture Store was running its annual sale. Karl was busy day and night.

Ruby sat alone in the park for hours and hours. Sometimes, she lingered near his store where she could see him through the window.

Ruby saw his mother, too. Like his, her eyes were long and brown, and her curly hair hung low on her neck. She wore silk shawls over her head. Gold earrings glistened in the lobe of her ears. From her fleet study of them, Ruby liked Karl's father but not Mrs. Strassburg. She didn't know why.

Ruby was peering through the window as Mr. Strassburg was trying to sell a bed. His wife drew her silken shawl about her head as she approached the customer. She gave her husband a quick contemptuous look. He stood aside as if in the habit of giving her the right of way. She pushed the bed to the light, felt the mattress and talked animatedly.

Ruby smiled as she looked on. The customer listened but did not want the bed, and slowly edged away as if fearing the woman's wrath. Mrs. Strassburg put a blue silk pillow on the bed, and turned on a floor lamp with a bright pink shade, and caught the customer's arm and led her back. The blue silk pillow under the glowing lamp had its effect. The customer hesitated and then smiled—and the bed was sold. Mrs. Strassburg gave her husband a sidelong look of contempt.

Then Ruby walked from the window. Maybe Karl had seen her. Maybe his parents had seen her. She lingered on the corner and then turned back. She would pass the store once more.

This time Karl saw her. He was in the window arranging candlesticks on a walnut dresser. He waved and beckoned her to wait.

"Ruby—Ruby!"

When he came outside she noticed how tired and hot he seemed.

"I'm sorry about today. I couldn't make it. This sale's been terrible. We sold over twenty sets of furniture."

He said the last with pride.

"The band was swell," she smiled indolently. "I listened to the violin like you said."

"Was he as good as last week?"

She nodded. "It was soft—like something floating in the air."

"I wish I'd been there."

"Can't—can't we go somewhere—tonight?"

"No, I'm sorry—we expect a lot of customers—

giving a silk pillow with every article we sell. I couldn't leave the store."

She didn't answer.

"But this sale'll be over soon and I'll be seeing you."

She struggled to conceal her disappointment. She had wanted so much to be with him. The evenings were so long and dull. And now another evening alone.

She wouldn't go home to Carrie and Nicki. She opened her purse and counted the change—nearly fifty cents, enough to go to the Chink's.

Karl was watching her quietly.

"What are you counting the money for?"

Her deliberate, careful gesture amused him.

"Gotta eat." She put the money back carefully and closed her purse.

"Going to eat alone?"

"Sure."

"What about your aunt? Won't she be expecting you?"

Ruby's eyes narrowed.

"I come home when I want to!"

"You're a swell kid, Ruby. So full of fight all the time. But I like that. You'll get ahead! You'll be something! I know it!"

He twirled his watch on its charm. "I wish I didn't have to work tonight. I'll be thinking all the time what you're doing—where you're going." He stopped. His watch fell against his wrist. "But after you eat—then what?"

"I dunno."

"You won't be lonesome, will you?"

"No."

"Why don't you go to a movie. There's a good one playing at the Unique. My father saw it last night—said it was great!"

"Does your father go all the time?"

"Sure, he does! He's the best customer the Unique has."

It occurred to Ruby that she liked Karl's father—was sorry for him. She thought of the buxom woman with the brilliant gold earrings who was Karl's mother.

"Does your mother go too, Karl?"

"No not often. She'd rather stay in the store." He returned his watch to his pocket and fished out a cigarette. "My mother can sell anything to anyone!"

"I know."

"How do you know?"

"I was lookin' in the window—I saw her sellin' a bed."

"You were looking in the window? I didn't see you!"

"You was busy— I saw you."

"Why didn't you come in?"

"I didn't want to buy nothin'."

"You don't have to buy anything to come in our place!"

"Guess your mother don't feel like that!"

Karl drew her nearer the lamp post light.

"What difference does it make what she thinks. I was there, wasn't I?"

"Sure."

"Next time you look in the window—come in!"

He held her hand in his. She liked the feel of his hand. It was firm and smooth and the finger tips were hard from the strings of his violin. Her throat quivered. She was a little ashamed of her feeling for him. She pulled her hand away quickly and clutched her purse. Then, unreasonably, it seemed, she laughed.

"You better go back—you mother'll be comin' out here!"

His eyes were riveted on her wide, brilliant mouth.

"Good-bye, Karl." She turned—her slim skirt fluttered from her knees.

He looked after her. There was seductive magic in her indolent shuffle. She would soon turn the corner and he wouldn't see her until another day.

"Ruby—Ruby!" He hurried after her. "Wait a minute!"

She stopped. And as she waited for him she noticed how, like his mother's, his curly hair fell on his neck.

"Ruby!" There was a dark flush on his face. "We've got to go out soon—like we did—that night."

"Sure!" She agreed simply. Her wide mouth was tantalizing. He caught her arm. She felt pleasantly captive.

"You won't go out with any other fellow to-night—will you?"

"I don't know no other fellows!"

Karl drew out his gold watch again, and twirled it confidently on its chain.

"That's right, Ruby—no one but me."

They were startled by a shrill call. It was Karl's mother calling him. Her face was restless, and her nervous hands were waving wildly. Her thin shawl lay folded awry on her shoulders.

"Karl! What's the matter with you—so long you stay away!" Her ever fluttering hands adjusted the shawl over her head. "You got better things to do than talk with a shiksa in the street!"

She turned into the store, her long skirt sweeping the sidewalk.

Karl flushed. "I guess I've got to go!"

He squeezed her unresponsive hand.

"Shiksa—that's what they call a Gentile girl."

Karl laughed uneasily. "Yes—a pretty Gentile girl!"

"Your mother don't like shiksas." Her pronunciation of the word was difficult. She said it as all pale blond Gentile girls pronounced it without color or richness. The word fell flat and strange and ridiculous on his ears.

"You say that word so funny, Ruby."

She didn't hear him. She was thinking of the florid woman, her waving nervous hands, her unfriendly eyes.

"Do Jews only go with Jews?"

"Don't be silly!"—furtively. "Good-bye—see you soon as I can, Ruby. You wait for me in the park—same bench." And he was gone.

She watched him hurry toward the store. His mother reappeared in the doorway and talked to him shrilly, in a strange language. Karl answered her curtly and disappeared.

Ruby didn't dare pass his window again that day. She walked quickly down June Street to the Chink's. In the window a festoon of red tissue paper rosettes surrounded a bright blue bowl with noodles. She counted her money again and entered.

Chapter XIII

Mrs. Strassburg was magnificent in the store. She outdid her husband and son. At night she switched on all the store lights and saw to it that the gold sign shone arrestingly from one end of June Street to the other.

"Look, Ben—the whole world will see our lights. We'll make good business tonight." She clucked her tongue and her earrings danced. "What would you do without me, Ben? What would you be?"

Her husband shrugged his shoulders and turned away. He had heard those words before, but they had long ago lost their effect on him.

"Some day Karl will have the store. What will you do without me, Karl?" She turned to her son. "I can't live forever."

"Don't talk that way, Ma. I don't want the store!"

"What! You like better to run around with that blond shiksa? I heard enough about you and her." And she turned from him, her silk shawl floating after her.

"Forget it, Ma! Why do you always have to talk like that!"

She regarded the youth reproachfully, with the

air of one deeply injured, martyred. And she wanted Karl to know how she felt.

"Don't talk no more, Karl. It is a pain in my heart. I have suffered all my life for you—and what will I have? Nothing—nothing! A son!" Mrs. Strassburg sat heavily on the green brocade couch. "A son!" She picked up the price tag—and glaring at her husband was all business again.

"Look, Ben! You are selling this couch for nothing! It's brocade! What's the matter with you? This couch don't go for one cent under twenty dollars!" She hastily changed the price, writing awkwardly with her left hand. Her wounded heart was forgotten entirely.

The green couch went that evening. Mrs. Strassburg sold it herself. She flipped the money before her husband's face and pushed him from the cash register arrogantly. Mr. Strassburg raised his solemn eyes to her.

"That's right, Sarah—what would I do without you?" He smiled dourly and retired into shadows among the beds, dining sets, and heavy brocades.

"You see, Karl—how I sell everything? And you don't want the store yet?"

Karl put his arm about her and patted her cheek.

"Don't talk like that, Ma. Sure, I want the store. I'm going to be a rich man. I'll buy you a seal coat with long tails, and a big house, and everything you want."

"Ya, Karl, ya—you'll get married—and I'll get nothing! That's always the way with children! What do they care what a mother has sacrificed?" Her eyes suddenly glistened with lurking tears, and her fingers fumbled with the necklace at her throat. "Ya, ya—I know!" She sighed and wiped her eyes.

"I'm not getting married for a long time, Ma. What do I want to get married for?"

"Sure, you'll get married, Karl—and to a nice Jewish girl. No blondie for my family, Karl!"

He didn't answer her. He knew his mother was thinking of Ruby. He had been thinking of her, too. He hadn't been able to get her pale face out of his mind. About him still lingered the fragrant smell of her powder. He still felt the warm clasp of her large, white hands. He still beheld her wide, brilliant mouth that so fascinated him.

"Why don't you answer me, Karl?"

His mother's cheeks were flushed and bright. He contemplated her. She must have been beautiful, his mother, long ago—with her long brown eyes, and her soft hair. She was almost beautiful now, but her figure had grown pudgy and her silken Oriental skin had coarsened. Only her hands were still beautiful— small, nervous, and deep olive. He stroked them tenderly, and they felt soft under his firm palm. He counted the rings on her fingers—old rings with diamonds. She always wore all her rings. It pleased her vanity. She liked to hear her friends say: "Mrs. Strassburg has got so many beautiful rings." It made her feel opulent and important. Only at night did she take them off. Karl had seen her tear them off hastily and push them under her pillow. In the morning they were always on her fingers, and she held her hands out and smiled over their perfection.

She interrupted his thoughts:

"You like your Ma, Karl—yes?"

"Sure, I do!"

"You're all I got, Karl—you're my whole life."

Karl laughed and looked at his father.

"You hear that, Pa? Ma says I'm all she's got!"

Mr. Strassburg nodded his head. "Ya—all she got." And then he walked from the store to take a smoke.

Mrs. Strassburg left Karl hastily to go over to a customer who wanted to buy a dining room set.

Karl watched his mother for a moment. She was doing well. She talked ingratiatingly and her face shone. She could be very pleasant, his mother, in times like this. She threw away the original price and made a new price for a new customer. She was like something magic. She stroked the fine wood in the table, and then she won.

Karl walked outside the store. It was getting late, and he was tired. He leaned against the door and lit a cigarette, and watched the people. Many stopped and looked into his window. He would be happy when this sale was over.

Another week—and then Ruby. Ruby! How could he wait another week to see her. He threw his cigarette away and looked at his watch. It was nearly ten. He went back into the store.

"How long do we keep open, Ma?"

"It's early yet. What's the matter?"

"I'm tired, Ma. We're not going to sell anything more tonight."

She waved a fist full of money in his face.

"Ya—you say that—you got some place to go. Ya?" She said shrewdly.

"No—no place special!"

"I know what you want to do. But we're not going to close yet." She rang the money up in the register.

The two Klein sisters had just come into the store. She went toward them smiling. Karl couldn't do better than a Klein sister—Mollie or Dora—it didn't matter which one. They were both eligible and pretty, and their father was a rich jeweler.

"Look, Karl—Mollie and Dora are here."

Karl went to greet them. They blushed and started to laugh.

"Hello, Karl! We came to buy some pillows!"

Their laughter tinkled through the store. At one time Karl had been interested in Dora, the one who spoke. She was the younger of the Klein sisters, and prettier than Mollie. She was dark and plump with a broad short nose, which had first attracted him. It didn't stamp her as a Klein. She might have been a Smith or a Henderson.

Mollie was taller and thinner, and wore thick glasses. She had finer skin than her sister, but she didn't have Dora's soft hair or her plump, round bosom. They both liked Karl, but he preferred Dora. The last time he had taken her to a dance was before he had met Ruby.

Karl picked up some silk pillows of bright rose and blues and showed them to the girls. Mollie examined them carefuly, but Dora looked at Karl.

"You think the rose one is better, Dora?"

Dora took the pillow from her sister and tossed it on the couch.

"What do you think, Karl?"

He didn't answer. He felt resentful and annoyed. He knew she hadn't come to buy pillows at all. Her laughter disturbed him. It jarred the picture of Ruby from his mind.

Dora picked up a blue pillow and tossed it beside the rose one.

"Do you like them together, Karl—the two colors?" She waited for his reply, anxiously.

"They look fine!"

But Mollie was not so easily satisfied. She selected

others, turning the pile upside down. Maybe Dora wasn't interested in buying pillows, but she was.

"Look, I got a green one—and only a dollar twenty-five!" Mollie came forward eagerly, her small eyes blinking behind her glasses—thick glasses, meant to correct her myopic tendencies, that only made her gaze more intent.

Dora was standing close to Karl and talking to him. She paid no attention to Mollie.

"Why don't I see you any more, Karl?"

"I've been busy, Dora." He was casual, too casual, and it cut her. Her young, heavy bosom rose under her dress.

"There's a dance in two weeks. You're going. Karl—aren't you?"

He shrugged his shoulders. His mind was a long way off. "Maybe—haven't thought of it."

"I've been asked by two fellows—but I didn't accept."

"Why didn't you?"

She broke into a giggle, and her skin was stained with a brilliant color.

"Because, there's someone else I'd rather go with!"

Karl understood, but said nothing. Mollie, who had gone to make her purchase, now came back to them and brought Karl's mother with her.

"Come over sometimes, girls. I never see you," said Mrs. Strassburg with meaning.

Dora, lingering back of Mollie, held out her hand.

"Good-night, Karl. Don't spend all your time in the park!"

He heard her laughter long after she had gone, and it sounded a trifle malicious.

His mother stood in the doorway beside him.

"Nice girl—Dora. So full of life."

He turned away. "Let's close now, Ma. It's nearly eleven."

"Ya—ya—your mamma's tired, Karl." Mrs. Strassburg began counting up the money in the cash register preparatory to going home. The end of the day had come. Karl put on his coat, and brushed his hair.

"Going to get a soda, Ma. I'll be home later."

She smiled and kissed his brow.

"Ya, Karl—hurry up—take Dora and Mollie. Maybe they would like one, too." She pushed him out of the door.

He sighed with relief when the cool air hit his face. He walked up the street, but he didn't follow Dora and Mollie. He was thinking of Ruby.

It was past eleven o'clock when he stopped at her door. There was an indefinable ache within him. Suppose she wasn't home at all—suppose she had gone out with some other fellow.

The blind was drawn in the back of the hat shop window, but he could see a light. Someone was at home! He rang the bell.

The door was opened almost at once. A huge woman stood in the doorway, dressed entirely in pink. She smelled of wine.

"What do you want?" She looked at him coquettishly.

His mouth felt dry. "Ruby—!"

"Who are you?"

"Karl Strassburg."

The pink lady became ingratiatingly friendly.

"Come on in, Karl. Ruby's in the parlor. My, won't she be glad to see you!" She took his arm and closed the door behind him.

Ruby was sitting under the orange lamp listening to Nicki sing. He was stretched out on the couch, waving his wine glass in tempo to his deep, rich voice. He was singing the Toreador song from Carmen.

"Look who's here, Ruby!"

Ruby turned and saw Karl. She seemed neither surprised nor pleased. But Nicki stopped in the middle of his song and lifted his shaggy head from the pillow.

"Why you come here?" His voice was thick from wine.

Karl stood awkwardly in the middle of the room, and its heat, the smell of perfume, oppressed him. He had often wondered how Ruby lived. He had never dreamed it would be like this. How could she have emerged so lovely and white from the dirty back room of a hat shop? He felt ashamed that he had come in on her like this.

"Karl, won't you have a drink?" Carrie said his name as though she had known him for years. It irritated him.

He looked helplessly at Ruby. She seemed not to care whether he went or stayed.

Nicki rose and came forward, swaying from side to side and looked at Karl belligerently. Ruby watched Nicki, and then, suddenly, she put down her glass and went to Karl. She had learned to suspect that sleek smile on Nicki's face.

"Want some air, Karl—too hot here." She slipped her arm through his. But Nicki interposed.

"Carrie no let you go out so late!" He tried to take her from Karl.

But quick as a wink she pushed the Greek back into a chair. The next moment she and Karl had left the room.

Carrie giggled and then stopped. There was a strange look on Nicki's face as if he had suddenly become ill. He threw the half filled glass to the floor and smashed it. The sweet Italian wine stained the rug and ran under the table; it looked as if someone had been killed.

Ruby was drunk. Karl hadn't noticed it until they

were outdoors. She swayed against him.

"Don't walk so fast," she said, clinging to his arm.

He did not answer. He was thinking of the way he had seen her in the parlor with Nicki. He was remembering her indifference.

"You weren't even glad to see me—tonight!"

"I was glad!"

"You just looked at me—I didn't know what to think."

"I didn't know you was coming!"

"You're drunk—" as she lurched against him.

"Nick brought in some new stuff he got on the wharf." Her eyes seemed dreamy. "I like to hear Nicki sing when he's drunk!"

The memory of the Greek singing to Ruby and getting her drunk infuriated Karl.

"What's this Greek to you, anyhow?"

Ruby laughed, that low throaty laugh of hers.

"My aunt's fellow."

"Seems to me he's crazy about you!" Fury was pounding inside him and it hurt. "You don't like him, do you?"

Her eyes narrowed viciously. "I hate him!"

Her animosity seemed to satisfy Karl. They walked on and on. The cool air cleared away some of the blur of the wine. It was midnight when they reached the bench in the park. They had walked through the lighted streets until the lights went out.

The park was deserted. Karl kissed her. He rubbed his cheek against her hands and held them to his heart.

"Feel how it pounds! That's what you do to me!"

She listened quietly to his heart. "Do I?"

"I could be with you forever, Ruby. Time doesn't matter to me at all." Then as he remembered Nicki: "That Greek! If he ever gets fresh with you—come to me!"

Her fragile, opal face looked like a blossom in the moonlight.

"Ruby—Ruby!"

He raised his brown, smooth face to hers. "This is a rotten town, Ruby—" he hesitated. "No place to go—no place at all!"

He touched the white frill of her blouse. Then he buried his troubled head in her throat.

CHAPTER XIV

THE next day Karl thought of everything that had happened the night before. He remembered how he had walked home through dark streets, and all the way the touch of her throat throbbed through him like an ache. He caught his breath quickly, and dug his nails into his palms. He could hardly stand the pain. He remembered her cheap, cotton blouse, falling loosely over her high breasts, white like her throat, white like her face. She must be white all over. Her long thin thighs, and her flat abdomen—all white, like cream.

Her aunt was white, too, but a dull pasty white like stale dough. He shuddered when he thought of her aunt and the Greek with the oily smirk. They were part of Ruby's life, but no part of Ruby, he was sure.

Then he remembered how he had found himself walking dazedly past his own house after he left her—only to stumble back again and find it.

His house was dark. He remembered how glad he had been. His mother and father were in bed. They were asleep in the wide bed with the down puffs. They had always slept in that bed. He had been born in that bed. His mother had loved and hated his father in that bed.

He had passed their door hastily and gone into his room. They would never know what time he had come in, or where he had been. He was relieved. He didn't have to lie. It was difficult to lie to his mother under her fixed, glittering eyes.

"You don't fool me, Karl—maybe papa—but not me!"

But he didn't have to lie to her last night when he took Ruby to the park. He didn't have to lie to her because his mother was asleep on the large bed with his father, her sleeping face with its smug smile turned away from the timid, quiet man she married long ago in a little town in Russia.

Then he thought of Dora Klein. His mother liked Dora. She liked all the Kleins. They were a good family with money. But Dora wasn't like Ruby. He used to like Dora's little feminine tricks, her cuddling manner, her baby pout. It used to amuse him when she came into the store on the pretense of buying something. She had come in last night to buy the pillows only to speak to him. He knew it. He was sure of it when she returned the silk pillow earlier that morning. She had fluttered about him, asking his advice. He had said nothing in reply. He had merely picked up another pillow and handed it to her. He had no interest in the sale. He had less interest in Dora. She watched him carefully.

"Do you think I'll look good against this color, Karl?"

"Sure, why not?"

"Oh, you haven't even looked!"

"You wanted this color, didn't you?"

"Well, isn't it the best for me?"

"I suppose so."

She pouted a little and draped herself on the couch and pushed the pillow in back of her head.

"Oh, I see—you don't like brunettes any more."

She giggled on a high malicious note.

"I know all about her, Karl—you can't fool me!"

She had said it just as his mother might have said it, and it startled him. His mother must have looked like Dora. Dora would look like his mother. She would wear that smug smile on her face when she grew older. The smug smile had already begun to take shape on her mouth.

"What's the matter, Karl? Have I done anything?"

"Don't be silly, Dora."

"Well, you don't ask me out any more—you don't come over to the house!"

"I've been busy—this sale—"

"But you've got time for other things!" She was defiant.

"What do you mean by that?"

"You know," she answered stubbornly.

Karl shrugged his shoulders. Dora's manner exhausted him.

"Aren't you going to the dance, Karl?"

"What dance?"

"The one I told you about—last night."

"I don't know."

She was coquettish again. "I'll be around in a few days and sell you a couple of tickets."

"All right, Dora."

Her eyes sparkled. "Will you really go, Karl?"

"If I'm not too busy here."

"Don't forget, I've already had two invitations." She looked up at him slyly. "But I'll give them both to Mollie."

"And what will you do?"

She hesitated a moment. "Maybe—maybe I'll get the one invitation I want!" And she walked swiftly from him and left the store.

It almost seemed to Karl that Dora and his mother were in league. Almost the first thing Mrs. Strassburg talked about when she reached the store was this dance.

"Have you bought tickets yet, Karl, for the Jewish dance?"

"Not yet—but I promised Dora I would."

Mrs. Strassburg clucked her lips together. "I want you should go. You'll have a good time!"

"But I don't want to go. I'll give the tickets to somebody else."

"I ask you, Karl—you should go."

"I'm sick of dances, Ma."

"But Dora wants you to take her."

"She doesn't have to worry about being taken. She always gets plenty of invitations!"

Mrs. Strassburg was exasperated. "Sure, she'll get plenty. What's the matter with you? Dora Klein is a nice girl. You'll never find a nicer one—and you're waiting yet so someone else should get her!"

"Who cares!"

"Who cares?" His mother shrieked. "I do. I want you should go with a nice Jewish girl! I don't want no blondies! I don't want no shiksas!"

Her hands cut the air like swords. Her voice was sharp and bitter. Mr. Strassburg tried to comfort her:

"What are you getting so upset for?"

"I shouldn't be upset, yet! He don't want to take Dora—and I shouldn't be upset!"

Mr. Strassburg was gentle: "There are other Jewish girls beside Dora. Maybe he don't like Dora so much." He put a restraining hand on his wife's shoulder.

She flung her husband from her. "Fool that you are! Dora is a girl from gold!"

Then she cried plentifully as she turned to Karl.

"Your papa don't care who you take—but, my son, you shouldn't break my heart!"

There it was, this distasteful threatening which exhausted and exasperated him. There was no contending against this.

He sighed. "You win, Ma. I'll take her."

His father smiled. "Sure you'll take Dora. Your mamma is right."

Mrs. Strassburg smiled, too. Her strategy had won.

The next day, Karl asked Dora to the dance. But he wondered what everyone would have said had he invited Ruby instead of Dora. He would be branded as a traitor to his own people. The boys would probably be pleased and vie to get every dance with her. The evening would be unbearable for all the Jewish girls. He'd show them! He'd bring Ruby!

He planned it maliciously. He would come in late with her. He would see that she wore her blue dress, and that her bangs were combed smoothly. He would dance every dance with her. He would smile triumphantly at Dora and lead Ruby over and introduce her. He laughed suddenly. He could see Dora's face color a deep crimson and her teeth bite into her soft lower lip. He liked to think of Ruby's cool, lazy manner which Dora could never understand. It would leave her bewildered and outraged. He flipped the tickets in his hand.

"Ma, suppose I didn't take Dora?"

His mother stopped abruptly and her hand went to her throat. "Are you maybe crazy or something? What kind of business is this, Karl?"

He smiled hopelessly. "Nothing—I just thought —maybe Dora couldn't go the last minute."

"Dora bought a new dress already! You shouldn't make monkey business!" Her eyes flashed angrily.

He took Dora.

"Oh, Karl, you dance so nice!" Dora repeated the phrase many times as they danced together. He only heard her once.

"You don't talk to me much tonight," she went on coyly. But there was bitterness underneath her simulated gaiety.

"It's so hot in here—let's go outside!"

She caught his hand. He didn't notice that her eyes narrowed when she led him outside to the balcony. "It's nicer out here, don't you think?" Then she hesitated: "I'm glad you asked me tonight, Karl." She leaned against him and her face was sultry.

He drew away and lit a cigarette.

"Having a good time, Karl?" She laughed to hide her embarrassment.

"Yes—are you?"

"Wonderful! But that's because I happen to be

with someone who—who—"

"You mean me?"

"Well—" there was a slight pause. "Someone who is a good dancer—and popular—and—"

"I used to like these dances."

"Don't you like them now?"

"Nothing happens at these affairs. They're all the same!"

She bit her lip and forced back the tears.

"You're not very nice to say that."

"I'm sorry—I guess I'm tired, that's all. This sale's been too much for me!"

"Who do you think you're fooling, Karl?—Not me!"

"I'm not trying to fool you, Dora."

"You think you're too good for all of us! You're so swell! And just because you happen to be a little better looking than the rest of the fellows!" Her anger rose to a point of hysteria, and then she sobbed. "I wish I had gone with someone else—someone who wouldn't think he was doing me a favor!" She bit out the words viciously, and then buried her face in her new chiffon handkerchief.

He stood by awkwardly. Her sobs were heavy and desperate. She was wounded to the heart. It was his fault. He put an arm about her. "I'm sorry I hurt you. I didn't mean to!"

She suddenly melted and offered her trembling

lips to him. He kissed her tenderly. She closed her eyes and caught her breath. Her tears were on his face.

Mollie and Herman Schmit burst out on the balcony. Karl dropped Dora quickly. Mollie giggled foolishly.

"So that's where you've been all evening. Mamma's been looking for you. So has papa."

Dora threw her sister a shrewd look. "Go and tell mamma not to worry."

Mollie went back to the dance floor with Herman.

"We'd better go back, too, Dora." Karl wasn't tender any more.

"I suppose so. Everybody'll wonder what became of us."

Karl refused to comment. Silently he led her away. Dora noticed that his hand barely touched her arm.

"That's the worst of a small town—you have to be so careful." She laughed gaily. It sounded forced and brittle to him. He realized that Dora could laugh as easily as she could cry.

Mrs. Strassburg watched her son and Dora come back into the hall. She was happy and her golden earrings danced in her ears. She followed them with her eyes as they waltzed together. She knew just how many times Karl had danced with Dora. She knew everything.

If the lilting melody of the waltz made Karl unhappy, it made Dora radiant.

"It's such a romantic song, isn't it, Karl?"

He nodded his head and thought of Ruby. He remembered the smouldering look in her eyes when
the band played that song—the night he heard her
sing it in her deep throbbing voice.

"What are you thinking of, Karl?"

"Nothing much!"

"Oh, yes you are, your face is so serious. I like you
best when you're full of fun—like you used to be."

She snuggled closer to him like a kitten, and her
silk dress rustled against him. Then the music
stopped, and the dance was over. But Dora still
clung to his arm.

That night, in the wide feather bed, Mrs. Strassburg didn't sleep with her back to her husband. She
was planning her son's future—she talked half the
night.

Chapter XV

Late Sunday morning, Nicki sat in Carrie's kitchen and watched her bathe her swollen feet in a pail of salt water. She was dressed in stiffly starched pink organdie, corseted and carefully rouged. The feet were evidently the last effort toward a meticulous grooming.

"My feet is killin' me, Nick," she groaned.

"You getting old, Carrie."

Her face quivered. "That's a swell thing to tell me."

"Why you have sore feet all time?"

"Because I shouldn'a wore those tight shoes last night—that's why! Besides, I'm all done out—workin' like I do—slavin' all the time." She started to whimper.

A frozen look came into Nicki's eyes. He liked to torment Carrie. "You getting old," he repeated.

"I'm just tired workin', Nick, that's all! I need a change—that's what's wrong."

"Sure—I know, Carrie. I like you. I no care you get old."

Carrie's eyes filled with tears.

"You make me seeck, Carrie—" he flung at her.

"Your eyes get all red. What Georgia say? Think I hit you, maybe. Hurry."

"I wish you could stay with me at Georgie's. She's havin' a swell dinner."

"Think I got nothing to do but stay at Georgia's."

She slipped into her stockings and shoes.

"I'm ready, Nick."

They went out to the car.

"I'll be missin' you, honey." Carrie snuggled close as they drove off. He tried to smile at her, but the lights in her amorous eyes deadened him. He was thinking of Ruby—Ruby back in the house they had left—Ruby alone.

The car came to a sudden stop in front of Georgia's house. Carrie made one more attempt to hold him.

"Georgia'll sure be mad cause you ain't staying!"

She edged herself laboriously out of the car, and shook out her ruffles.

"How do I look, Nick?"

"Like hell, Carrie," he smiled oilily. She almost wept. Then she accepted his smile.

"Don't forget to come back for me, Nick."

He left her hastily, relieved that he wouldn't have to see her ridiculously painted face any more that day. He was eager to go back to the house and find Ruby!

Chapter XVI

She was asleep when Nicki opened the door to her room. He saw her yellow hair draped on the pillow. Her arms were flung over her forehead and hid her eyes. He could see her mouth, wide and lovely. He called her name:

"Ruby!"

Languidly, she stirred on the pillow. Her lazy mouth parted a little and showed the edges of her sharp teeth. Ruby was something for a man like Nicki. He wanted someone white and soft and vicious.

"Ruby!"

She started in her sleep. Her arm fell listlessly across her breast. Nicki blew the smoke from his cigarette in her face. It hovered over her like a descending veil.

"Ruby!" Her name was like fire in his mouth.

He touched the clothes she had worn the night before—lifted them gently and held them to his face. They smelled of her skin.

Ruby slowly opened her eyes. She lay quietly for a moment. Then, as she saw Nicki, her eyes narrowed like a cat's ready to spring.

"What the hell you doin' in my room?"

He shrugged his silk-sheathed shoulders carelessly.

"I come to play nice music to wake you up."

"You got a rotten nerve comin' in here!"

Nicki ignored her anger, put on a record, and hummed the song that came from the phonograph on her dresser.

"Turn that thing off!"

"Sure, baby—anything you say." He turned it off, and all the time his eyes were riveted upon her.

"Now get out of here, you big wop!"

He laughed as he bent to her face and touched her rumpled hair as if the strands were gold.

"Why you call me wop all the time? I'm Greek. Nicki, the Greek. I come to take you out today. I get boat—we take nice ride on river."

Ruby scowled. "Where's my aunt?"

"She go over to see Georgia. Maybe Georgia expect another baby—who knows? Bill home all the time now!"

"I ain't goin' with you!"

There was something evil in his slumberous eyes. "You go with me, baby—Nicki want you to go!"

"Get out of here, Nick!" She picked up her slipper. It dangled dangerously in her hand. He laughed.

"What you do with pretty slipper?"

She clutched it tightly. "Get out of here! Do you hear?" She raised the slipper over her head and buried the sharp heel in his cheek, lacerating it. He gritted his teeth and held his breath for a moment.

"You are like little cat, Ruby." He rubbed his hand over the wound. The pain of it was sharp and luxurious. "Nicki like little cat. You come with me today. I buy you anything you like."

"I'll tell my aunt about you!"

His eyes appeared as narrow as two slender cuts. "What I care if you tell her! She's not here, now." Then he grabbed her to him. "You no hate me, Ruby!"

"Let me go!"

She breathed with difficulty and tried to wrench his hands from her naked shoulders. She couldn't.

"I give you good dinner—plenty wine—you be happy, and I sing nice music!" He breathed in her hair. "I crazy about you, baby—for a long, long time." He pushed her down on the bed. "Maybe I no want to go for boat ride after all—baby."

Ruby was breathless and her hands were cold as ice. She was thinking fast. She would have to trick Nicki. She would have to get him out of the room somehow.

"Listen, Nick—I'll go with you. I like a good time once in a while. I'll go in the boat."

His hands tightened on her shoulders. "Maybe you fool me, baby?"

"No, Nick—why do you think that?"

He picked up her stockings, her teddy. "Show Nicki how you get dressed."

Ruby saw that there was something unhealthy about his pallor, something cruel in his lustful eyes.

She pulled up her stockings, conscious that his eyes were studying her. She slid her legs under the bed:

"You better go if you want me to get dressed."

"You think you get rid of Nicki?" he asked her suspiciously. She laughed. "I ain't goin' with you if you don't let me dress."

He was silent a moment. Then he wet his lips and started for the door. He turned suddenly:

"I wait for you on the corner."

"I'll be there, Nick—" as the door closed on him.

Her heart stopped beating. She had tricked Nicki after all. She fell back against the pillows exhausted. Then she rose hastily and locked the door. She would never go with him. She would go out through the alley and across the fence. She remembered that Karl had told her to come to him if Nicki bothered her. She would go to the park and find him.

She pulled the nightgown over her head. She took down her blue dress from the closet. It was the one that Karl liked.

Ruby hurried out. She hugged the doorways and walls, carefully picking her way from the alley to the street, swiftly and silently as the yellow cat that nocturnally ruled the domain.

Quickly she turned the corner. She was now a block away from the hat shop. Safe! Though her knees were going numb, the fear of Nicki kept her going. She hurried almost stumbling up the street, and somehow in spite of her haste, her feet seemed weighted to the pavements.

Only one thought pounded through her brain. She must see Karl! He would be waiting for her in the park. Together they would listen to the music and she would be safe and happy. Happy!

She crossed the street and hurried past the Empire Hotel. She could see the park. She could hear the music. Nicki passed out of her thoughts.

She was about to hurry through the park entrance to seek the bench—their bench—when Nicki loomed up before her. His sleek smile was smooth and fixed.

"You think you fool Nicki, baby?" He laughed. "I know you come here to find that boy—so Nicki come here, too!"

She could hardly answer him. The suddenness of his appearance froze the words on her lips. She tried to walk past him, but he stood in her way as he used to do when she went to school in the mornings.

"You don't like go in boat with Nicki—so Nicki come to park to hear music with you." He gripped her arm. His smile was gone. There was menace in his voice.

"You never get away from Nicki, baby—never!"

Her fear of him returned. "I ain't goin' to sit with you."

He laughed melodiously. "Sure you sit with me, and that boy get one pain when he see you with Nicki!"

"I ain't goin' to, Nick."

He grabbed her arm again. He led her through the park. She was held close by him, helpless in his grasp. She threatened, speaking through her teeth:

"I'll tell my aunt—you'll see—I'll tell Karl!"

He held her tighter.

"What I care you tell her! And Karl—I break his neck some time! Nicki no afraid for him!"

Karl was sitting in the park with the Klein sisters when Nicki and Ruby passed. His eyes followed her anxiously. He saw Nicki find a bench and draw Ruby into the seat beside him. He felt so helpless just then with Dora saying maliciously:

"There goes your friend, Karl. Who's she with?"

She winked at Mollie. Mollie settled her thick glasses and peered at Ruby. She took the cue from her sister:

"She's got a new flame—I suppose came to the park to hear the music."

"She loves music," Karl was furious. What was Nicki doing in the park with Ruby? Why had she come with him? Why? Dora's voice jarred him again:

"Isn't that the Greek who has the fruit stand?"

Mollie spoke at the same time: "She doesn't look like the type that comes to the park just to hear music."

"How do you know, Mollie?"

"I know her type," Dora smiled sweetly. "You can't fool us!"

"You don't know anything about her, Dora!"

She flushed, and the smile left her face.

"I know why a Jewish boy bothers with a girl like that!"

"She's awfully pretty, though—that girl," Mollie turned her thick glasses onto Karl questioningly.

Her sister cut in: "I don't think so. Look at her terrible clothes!"

Mollie was kinder. "Every girl can't dress as well as we do, Dora. Papa's rich—it's different."

Dora was annoyed at the way the conversation was going. Mollie was so stupid.

Karl tried to avoid looking at Ruby, but he couldn't. The band started another number. The music started to rise and fill the air with melody. Karl watched Ruby's face. Dora watched Karl's as she shifted on the bench. The music didn't interest Dora.

"What time is it?" Karl was uneasy. He tried to

see the watch on Dora's arm. She held up her arm to him with the solid gold watch. No other girl in St. Marks had a watch like that—all set with jewels.

Karl sighed. It would be an hour before the concert was over. Hopelessly, he longed for the courage to leave Dora and go to Ruby. But some strange loyalty kept him beside Dora—a girl of his own race. She had made him promise to give her the whole afternoon. How he hated her persistent saccharine ways!

"What are you going to do after the concert, Karl?" She was shrewdly planning the evening.

"I haven't thought about it."

"Well—it's such a lovely ride to the beach—and—"

"Not tonight, Dora. I'm tired!"

She drew her mouth into a baby pout. Her eyes were spiteful and hurt.

"Oh, I see. Well, a Jewish girl can't be as popular as some Gentiles, I know. There's a reason! But she's got that Greek with her—maybe she'll turn you down."

Karl was miserable. Maybe Ruby was going somewhere with Nicki. Maybe she was fond of Nicki, after all. Hadn't she told him that Nicki loved music—how he sang to her?

He sat for a long time, and he was wretched. He couldn't endure Dora's and Mollie's chatter. He couldn't endure the agony that tore at his heart when he saw Nicki smile into Ruby's face.

"Let's go home, Dora, the concert's nearly over." There was determination in his manner as he got up from the bench and walked Dora and Mollie from the park.

There was the suggestion of a faint smile on Dora's lips as she looked back and saw Ruby and Nicki staring at them.

"You see—what he do to you, Ruby!" Nicki was triumphant.

Ruby was numb and cold, without any feeling for anything. She felt only a dull ache as she followed Karl with her eyes and saw him go off with the two girls.

"Nicki is better to you—yes? He take you to eat. He buy you fine dinner—yes?"

"I don't want nothin', Nick!"

He laughed good-naturedly. "Sure you want something. Nice wine—good steak—apple pie—box choc'lates. And then, later, when it is night—we go for a ride on the water, baby."

"No, Nick—nothin'."

She bit her lip and scraped her shoes in the dirt and kept thinking of Karl.

Up in the band stand, the musicians were preparing to leave. People were leaving. She didn't want to be alone with Nicki in the park.

"Let's get out of here, Nicki."

He rose eagerly, and caught her arm. She edged away from him. He saw her gesture and laughed. They walked to the entrance of the park. There was an expression in Ruby's face as if all interest in life had left her.

"Don't be sad, baby. You too good for that boy, Karl."

She didn't answer. She was thinking Karl didn't care any more. He had found another girl—one of his own race.

"You want popcorn, Ruby?" Nicki stopped at a vender's cart and bought her a large bag. He bought her peanuts, too, and bright pink slabs of candy.

"Nicki buy you everything, baby—everything."

She took his presents indifferently. She held them in her hands but didn't eat. She was not even conscious of Nicki just then.

But the Greek was happy. He talked volubly and told her of his plans. Tonight a ride on the river. And wine. Tomorrow a new dress—a nice new dress with bright buttons and ribbons—and maybe lace petticoats. Nicki could spend money all right.

"Hear what I say, baby?"

She stopped suddenly and the presents dropped from her hands and spilled on the grass.

"Look, Nicki." She said it proudly as she saw Karl hurrying toward her.

Karl went to Ruby at once. He paid no attention to the Greek.

"I was afraid you wouldn't be here—when I got back!"

The vague look in Ruby's eyes had faded. She was so happy he had come back. She tried to tell him so, but the words were stifled in her throat.

Nicki pushed Karl away from Ruby. His eyes blazed with fury.

"You get out of here! We no want you! You got other girl!"

"That isn't true, Ruby. I couldn't help it to-day—" he was pleading with her.

Nicki laughed harshly, mirthlessly. "How she know that! You no good! I break your bloody neck! That's what I do!"

His voice rose in anger. The veins in his face looked swollen and full of blood. His eyes were shot with red streaks. "You get out of here!"

Already his angry words had attracted people to them. They stood hesitantly on the sidelines and watched curiously. They wondered how this slender Jewish boy would come out in a fight with the stocky Greek. They wondered about the blond girl with the torn paper bags of candy at her feet.

"I break your bloody neck!"

Nicki moved threateningly toward Karl.

The crowd started to murmur, but no one came

forward to intercede. Some Jewish girls who knew Karl joined the group of onlookers.

"Why, it's Karl! What's happened?"

He heard his name. He saw his friends. Misery and embarrassment filled him.

Nicki's eyes blazed with murder.

"You coward! You dirty coward!"

Ruby pushed herself between the two men. Tightly, she clutched Karl by the arm, and walked off with him. Two or three men held onto Nicki. The crowd murmured again. The Jewish girls called Nicki a dirty wop and spat at him.

Ruby and Karl walked together silently until they were far off from the park. Then Karl spoke:

"I know how you felt when you saw me with Dora. I don't blame you—but my mother gets ideas sometimes—"

She mumbled awkwardly: "I know."

She didn't blame him for spending his afternoon with Dora. Dora was of his race. Jews always stuck together. Her aunt had told her that.

Ruby remembered how Carrie had spent a whole summer once with a short Jewish man who sold men's union suits. His name was Maxie. Once he gave her a gold watch that she pinned on her blouse and put his picture inside. Then his wife came to town with her two boys, and Aunt Carrie was left alone. That was a long time ago, when Ruby was only a little girl, but the gold watch still clung to Carrie's massive bosom—and she still kept Maxie's picture inside. Ruby could hear her say:

"Jews is funny—give you presents—and give you a good time—but they always stick to their own kind."

Ruby wondered if Karl was like Maxie. But no— Karl could never be like that. Karl was young, and thin, and he loved music. Maxie only loved the night, when he could sit in the room with Carrie and eat liverwurst sandwiches, and count up his orders for men's union suits. Karl loved music, and she loved music. Karl wasn't like Maxie!

"Did you hear what they played today, Karl?" she had forgotten about Dora—about Nicki.

"Didn't hear very much of it." He ran his fingers through his hair as he always did when he was tense and nervous. "I was thinking of you all the time."

He looked up and saw her smile. It was beautiful. She had forgotten everything.

"Let's go somewhere. I want to hear about this Nicki." He took her hand. She followed. The streets were deserted and cold. He walked silently—silently. Then he stopped in front of his store—unlocked the door, and they went in together.

Inside, she looked about her with a fastly beating heart.

"We're alone, Ruby," Karl whispered.

For a moment they stood there in the darkness. The furniture took on weird positions, wooden silhouettes that seemed to stand on guard. They were like odd shaped people, grimly conscious of her invasion upon their solitude.

"You got a lot of furniture," she looked about curiously. She was glad she wasn't alone.

"Come here, Ruby." Karl took her in his arms and held her to him desperately. Then he slipped to the floor and buried his head on her knees.

She touched his shoulder. He was trembling and warm.

"We can't go on like this." His voice was broken, choked. "I—I love you!"

She stood very quietly. She didn't know what to say to him. He pleaded: "Why don't you say something to me, Ruby?"

But she couldn't talk—couldn't say anything.

"Ruby—I—I—"

Then he rose to his feet and walked to the window and drew the blind. The room was almost black. He had shut out the world. No one could take her from him, now. Not his mother! Not Dora! No one!

"Ruby!" Her name sounded strange in the darkness. "Do you love me?"

She didn't answer. She was listening to his voice. It was deep like music, and it stirred something in her. He took her in his arms and carried her to the carved walnut bed with the silk spread. He placed her on it.

It felt like the most beautiful spread in the world to Ruby, but she couldn't see the color. Karl had even shut out the moon. She was glad he had shut out the moon. She couldn't see the stiff, wooden pieces made so expertly in the Strassburg Furniture factory and appearing so hideous in the dark.

"I love you so much."

She didn't see the rapture in his face when he whispered those words. She touched his mouth. He kissed her fingers.

"You're so beautiful—" Then his voice died.

Ruby lay silently on the lustrous spread on the carved walnut bed.

She never saw that bed again. She never knew the color of the spread. Mrs. Strassburg sold them both the next day.

CHAPTER XVII

THE same thing happened to the red plush couch. It stood in the window of the Strassburg Furniture Store for almost a week. It was priced twenty-two fifty. Then, suddenly, it was sold. Karl told her it had been newly decorated with gold braid and the price changed.

"Who bought it, Karl?" Her voice fell like ice in the darkness of the store. And as she spoke to him, he thought to himself how much he loved her. He must have fallen in love with her long before he even knew her. She asked him the same question again. He finally answered:

"What difference does it make who bought it?"

"I want to know—that's all."

"You're a funny girl—sometimes." He took her in his arms and held her close. "But you're my girl, Ruby."

"Who bought it, Karl?"

"Why do you always ask that question? I don't care who bought it."

"Who bought it, Karl? Think—"

If he hadn't loved her so much, the monotonous persistence of her question would have wearied him.

"I guess a woman bought it—maybe a Polack—they like red, don't they? Maybe a Greek. I don't know!" He lit a cigarette. "We sell lots of furniture. You don't expect me to remember every piece, do you?"

"No, Karl."

"We're a big firm, you know—lots of customers."

"I know."

He ground out his cigarette in the red lacquered tobacco stand. The smoke died in one thin line. Ruby watched it quietly. She was thinking that something inside her was melting away like the smoke. She was thinking she'd never see the red plush couch again, either. It had been taken out of her life forever.

"Do you remember the green painted bed, Karl?"

"Which one?"

"The one I liked—the one that was sold. Do you remember it?"

He hesitated, but her eyes were fastened on him. He couldn't evade the fierce look in them.

"Let me see—oh, yes—I remember now. Ma sold it to a man from nigger town."

Ruby gasped. "You let her sell it to a nigger?"

"His money is as good as anyone else's."

"But that bed—*ours!*"

Ruby was silent and sad. The pale green bed was beautiful. It had delicate thin legs like a dancer. It was not made for a black man and his wife!

They were silent for a long time—each going his own way in thought. Then Karl suddenly said:

"Someday, things will be different. Someday, Ruby—you wait and see—we're going to be married. Then we won't have to steal in here at night—and be careful all the time. We won't have to do that!"

"I like this store at night—it's so quiet."

"I hate it! I hate this furniture! Smells of varnish and paint! Gives me the creeps at night!"

"Why—?"

"I don't know. I'm afraid someone might come in. Suppose someone did try to come in, Ruby—what would we do?"

"I ain't afraid of no one."

He lit another cigarette nervously. The small point of light shone on his face. It was drawn and smooth. It had the appearance of satin ready to split.

"I ain't afraid of Nicki—or Carrie—"

"That Greek—he doesn't know?"

She shrugged her shoulders. "Ain't said nothin'."

Karl sighed gratefully. Ruby whispered:

"Don't you worry about nothin'."

"I'm not worrying."

"Honest?"

"Sure. I've got you—haven't I?"

There was an absence of sincerity in his voice.

Ruby knew it. She knew it every time they stayed together in the darkness. She could feel his heart beat furiously whenever they heard anyone pass the store.

"Listen to that laugh, Ruby."

"No one ain't goin' to come in."

Her casual tone always gave him courage.

"I know—I know. I'm only afraid someone will find out about us."

But nobody found out. Not Nicki. Not Carrie. Not Karl's mother with her beautiful, nervous hands and her sharp eyes. Ruby wondered what Carrie would say if she found out. She seemed to know.

"Got a rich Jew—ha!—think you're somethin'." Then she would pull the strings of her corset tighter, and her face would get red like fresh liver, and her breath would come in gasps. "What you get out of it, that's what I'd like to know?" Carrie always wanted a bangle for her affection. Carrie was smart. She told Ruby that over and over. "Get somethin'— that's business." Ruby never said anything. She thought to herself, there weren't many bangles in Carrie's life now.

Karl had given Ruby a gold ring with a blue stone and he had said: "The stone is the color of your eyes." She loved the ring. She never once thought of it as a bauble.

That night when she came home, she showed the ring to Carrie. Her aunt sat up in bed eager to appraise it. She turned it this way and that. Then she laughed raucously.

"A swell thing to get from a rich Jew!"

"What you laughin' at?"

But Carrie went into another spasm of mirth. She rolled back and forth on the bed and let out fearful sounds of glee.

"A swell thing, all right! A ring with a cheap blue stone. Ain't worth beans!"

"It's gold—ain't it?"

Carrie looked at the ring contemptuously.

"Makin' fun of me!" Ruby's face had a fierce look. Carrie was afraid of Ruby when she looked like that. She pulled the covers up close to her neck and edged away from her. She gave her back the ring.

"I ain't makin' fun of you."

"Laughin' at me!"

"Go on—git to bed." Carrie was anxious to have Ruby go. She was still afraid.

"This is a swell ring—say so!"

"Gold and brass looks the same to me—same color."

"This ain't brass!"

"Maybe—"

"This is gold!"

"How I know what it is?"

"You know!"

"Go on, now—I want to sleep!"

Carrie closed her eyes wearily. But Ruby wouldn't let her go back to sleep. She shook her, determined to make Carrie open her eyes, to admit that the ring was beautiful. She hadn't forgotten the morning Carrie had told her she wasn't smart because she wouldn't take a lace teddy from Red after he tried to get out of giving it to her.

"Open your eyes."

She shook her aunt again.

"Say—it's gold!"

"What you botherin' me for? I don't care about your ring."

Ruby still held Carrie's shoulder with a firm hand.

"Sure, you care! You want me to get things! You told me so yourself!"

Carrie's hands fumbled nervously with the frills on her nightgown. She whimpered:

"You got no feelin's, Ruby. Always pickin' on me—sayin' things I never said."

"You said it! You and Nick said I ain't smart!"

Carrie sobbed pathetically.

"Course you're smart—smart as a whip. I always said—"

"You're a liar!"

"No, I ain't, Ruby—I ain't!"

Carrie's tears ruined the color on her face.

"I always knew you could get anything you want from a man."

Ruby eyed her steadily.

"I never asked Karl for this ring."

"He likes you, Ruby. He's rich."

Ruby's face darkened. "Karl ain't like your Maxie."

"Maxie was all right!"

"Maxie was soft and fat like butter."

Carrie's eyes bulged. She was the angry one now. Her skin was blotchy and livid with fury.

"Don't you say nothin' 'bout Maxie!"

"Maxie gave you an old locket with his picture inside. I remember—"

"And Karl gave you a cheap gold ring—for what?"

Carrie rose in her bed, throwing the covers from her. She lunged toward Ruby. Her voice was tight and choked:

"You little cat!"

She struck out at Ruby furiously. Ruby jammed her back against the iron bed. Carrie screamed and fell with a thud.

The next night Ruby gave the ring back to Karl. She couldn't put out of her mind what Carrie had said.

"Don't you like it, Ruby?"

"I don't want it, Karl."

He didn't speak for a moment. There was bewilderment in his eyes. Only Ruby didn't see his eyes.

The store was too dark. But she heard the hurt quality of his voice when he finally said:

"All right, Ruby—just as you say." He put the ring in his vest pocket. "I'm sorry. I thought you'd like it."

"I like it, Karl." But she couldn't explain to him that something in her revolted against taking the ring from him. She wanted it—but she couldn't take it. She loved beautiful things—things that shone—things made of gold. She had been proud of the ring yesterday—but she didn't want it today—because of Carrie.

"Karl—it's a pretty ring. I—"

She wanted him to know she wasn't like Carrie. She wanted to tell him she could never let him be like Maxie. She wanted to tell him, but she couldn't.

Chapter XVIII

Mrs. Strassburg found the ring in Karl's pocket. She closed her hand on it quickly, tied it up in her handkerchief and hid it in her purse. She turned to her husband.

"Ben—Karl's going around with that girl again!"

Her eyes flashed like diamonds, and she clasped her hands desperately together. Her gentle husband only smiled a little sadly.

"Ben! Say something! Did you hear what I told you? He's going around with that blond girl again!"

He puffed at his cigar slowly and nodded his head.

"I heard you."

"Then say something! *Say something!*" Her voice rose excitedly.

But he only smiled his patient, tender smile and puffed once more at his cigar.

"Nu—what is there to say?"

"What is there to say! What is there to say!" She screamed the words at him. "Ben, you think it's nothing he's going around with that girl?"

Mr. Strassburg knew that anything he might say would only disturb his wife more. With a troubled look on his face he walked to the front of the store.

But she followed him, hurling bitter words as she went. They had no effect; he had heard them so many times in so many years.

She pulled the handkerchief from her purse and waved it triumphantly in front of his eyes.

"Ben, he bought for her a ring. Do you know what that means, when he buys her a ring?" She opened the knot of the handkerchief and showed him the little gold ring with the blue stone.

"Where did you find it?" He was interested at last.

"Nu—so you didn't believe me! I found it in his pocket!" She clamped her mouth tightly together.

"Maybe he bought it for Dora."

His theory maddened her. She was in the midst of a tragedy and he was going to ruin it. She knew Karl. She knew he had bought it for Ruby.

Ruby—Ruby with the blond hair who walked by the store and looked into the window. She had seen her so many times. She had watched her shrewdly as she had watched Karl. She saw her son look at the girl furtively and talk to her with his eyes through the glass window. She had seen him watch Ruby anxiously when she turned from the window and walked down the street. She saw it all clearly. Karl was in love with this Gentile. He didn't want Dora. He wanted Ruby.

"Ben, we gotta do something!"

"Ya—ya."

"Ben, we can't let him marry this Gentile. It's a disgrace, Ben—it's a shame!"

"Ya—ya."

He mumbled the same words over and over in a dreary tone. She broke down and buried her face in her beautiful hands.

"He has fights in the street with that Greek her aunt lives with. Everybody saw him—and that girl! —he wants that girl yet!"

Mrs. Strassburg was ashamed of her son. She had heard about Nicki and the quarrel in the park. She cracked her hands in agony.

"Doraleh is a wonderful girl, Ben!"

"Ya—ya."

"He must marry Doraleh, Ben!"

"Ya—ya."

"My heart is breaking, Ben!"

Mr. Strassburg looked down at his wife tenderly. Then he turned away and took another cigar from his pocket.

"Ben! I'll tell Karl something! He'll hear from me!" She clutched the purse to her with the ring. "He'll hear from me!" she cried again.

"Ya—ya!"

It seemed all her husband could say—all he dared say.

She wiped her eyes and threw back her head. The

earrings jumped in her ears. She could fight Ruby! Ruby—who waited for him in the park. Dora had told her that—Dora who loved Karl and wanted him. Dora who was rich and strong and pretty. Dora had told her, and she had cried a little.

Mrs. Strassburg adjusted her shawl in the mirror of a walnut dresser. She hid the purse under the mattress. And then she smiled. A man with a fat pocket book had just come into the store. She knew the size of his bank account. Mrs. Strassburg always smiled when she was sure of good business.

All that day she watched Karl, but remained silent. She was waiting for the late evening to come when the store was quiet to show him the ring. She wondered what he would say to her when she told him she knew all about this blond girl, and she could hardly wait for the day to pass. The words were on her tongue so many times. She felt she could not wait a moment longer to tell him what she knew. But she fought them back and waited until they were ready to close the store.

It was a long day—the longest day in Mrs. Strassburg's life. When the last customer had gone she pulled out the bag from under the mattress.

"Time to go, Ma—isn't it?" Karl was putting on his coat. He looked at his watch. It was nearly eleven—almost time to meet Ruby.

But Mrs. Strassburg wasn't going home yet. She

sat down on a couch and remained grim. Her husband waited to see what would happen. He didn't know why, but he felt sorry for his son.

"Good business today—wasn't it, Ma?"

His mother held her lips tightly together. She was waiting for her husband to go.

Mr. Strassburg understood. He looked at his wife. There was a silent, potent language between them. He knew every flicker that passed over her face. He knew when she wanted him to stay—and he knew when she wanted him to go. He never questioned her authority. He merely glanced at her, and understood. So, now, he walked to the back of the store and left them alone.

"Karl—I found something."

She opened her purse—she untied the handkerchief slowly and let the ring roll into her lap. She picked it up in the palm of her hand and showed it to him.

"Karl—how can you do such a thing? How can you do this to your mother?"

Her emotion choked the words in her throat. They came to Karl muffled and sobbing. He felt his own throat tighten—but not with pity for his mother's anguish. Ruby! His mother had Ruby's ring!

He looked around the store dully. Their store— Ruby's store. It didn't seem so dusty, so dismal, so cluttered at night when he was alone with Ruby. It wasn't so damp and stale at night. It was warm and dark and filled with the smell of Ruby's perfume. Ruby's ring! His hand went quickly to his vest pocket.

"Karl—my heart is broken!" His mother had not ceased to talk. "Karl, how can you do such a thing?"

"Do what, ma?"

"You know, my son."

She clutched his hand and kissed it many times. Karl sighed wearily, hopelessly. There was nothing he could say.

"You didn't buy this ring for Dora! Why don't you go with a Jewish girl? Why do you break my heart? Why do you have to bring disgrace upon me?"

He didn't answer her. Ruby! She had Ruby's ring! He loved Ruby—and he wanted to tell his mother he couldn't help it that she wasn't born to their faith.

"Why—why do you bring disgrace upon me!"

"I'm not bringing disgrace to you, ma."

She cried in her beautiful hands. Her sobs were deep and heavy as if her heart was being torn out.

Karl was silent. It embarrassed him to see his mother broken by her grief. He wanted to comfort her. But the thought of Ruby gnawed at him.

"Ma, you shouldn't cry like this."

She lifted her face to his. It was red and swollen.

"I have much to cry about, my son—you have brought disgrace upon me!"

"I haven't disgraced you, ma."

"My father was a Rabbi—his father's father was a Rabbi. We have been honored people, Karl. What have we done to God that He should punish us like this!"

"I haven't done anything to disgrace you."

"Yes—yes—my son! You're going with this girl! I saw her myself looking through this window— waiting for you to come out of the store. I saw her!"

Her tears had dried on her cheeks. There was a strange madness in her eyes. Her hands rose above her head and fluttered in agony in the air.

"I will kill myself, Karl—if you marry her! I tell you—I will kill myself!"

Her voice rose in a frenzy, and a weird bright color stained her bloodless face. Karl was struck by her words. He had to reassure her in some way.

"But I'm not marrying her, ma."

"Yes—yes—you want to marry her! You bought for her this ring! She wants to marry you! And, why not? Aren't you Strassburg's son? Aren't you rich? Wouldn't you make her a good husband!"

"But I'm not thinking of marriage," he lied.

Her frenzy stopped for a moment. She peered into his eyes.

"But I want you to get married—I want you to marry a nice Jewish girl—and have good children—and live a good life!"

"But there's lots of time for that."

"No, Karl. I married Papa when I was only sixteen—we built together the business—Papa and me. You and Dora could be happy together."

The mention of Dora's name infuriated him.

"But I don't want Dora. I told you a hundred times already. I don't want her!"

Her eyes flashed with anger. "Karl, you will bring me to my grave! I don't want this blond shiksa!"

He clenched his hands furiously. He felt a sickness in his heart—a dull, heavy pain in his flesh.

"She's so beautiful, ma—so wonderful. You don't know her."

Mrs. Strassburg grabbed his arm.

"What!—you say that to me! You are bringing disgrace to me in my life—disgrace to me when I die. They will not bury me in a grave with honored people. I will be set apart, and a black wall will keep me from the other world—a black wall because my son married a Gentile!"

She wailed and cracked the bones in her hands, swaying back and forth on the couch in an agony of woe.

Karl looked at her darkly. At the moment he felt almost hatred for her—his mother who had brought him into the world, a Jew. Why couldn't he have been born into the world to Ruby's faith? Why—why? What law was there that said he must not marry Ruby! What creed was there that could tear her from him!

He looked at his mother, so broken, so crushed, huddled pathetically on the couch. He didn't hate her—he loved her! But he loved Ruby, too. He buried his face in his hands, and tried to dull the pain that struck at his heart. He felt so futile, so helpless, so miserable.

Slowly, Mr. Strassburg walked from the back of the store to where his wife and his son were. His heart ached for both of them.

"Karl, my son—mamma only wants you should be happy."

Karl didn't answer. Mr. Strassburg turned to his wife:

"Mamma—he ain't married her yet."

She held up a trembling hand to her husband.

"You say that when he bought this ring for that girl?"

There was something in Mr. Strassburg's manner that soothed and caressed and tenderly enfolded them both. Karl turned to his father.

"Where did ma get it—the ring?" He could not believe his mother had gone through his clothes to discover it.

Mr. Strassburg shrugged. Karl held out his hand to his mother.

"Give it to me, ma."

She laughed in his face, hysterical again.

"You want to give it to her—you can't fool your mother, Karl! You can't fool me!" She trembled and shook. Then she threw the ring to the floor and ground it under her shoe.

Karl watched her, and he clenched his hands together until the flesh was white and drawn. He fought back the desire—the maddening desire to strike her down. Fury welled in his heart—and then died.

"I'm going, pa." He turned on his heel and went out.

Mrs. Strassburg stood where he had left her crushing the little ring—crushing it as though she were crushing Ruby's face, and marring her beauty forever.

Mr. Strassburg walked sadly up and down beside his wife, watching her fury, and every now and then he said sadly:

"Mamma—mamma."

CHAPTER XIX

MRS. STRASSURG brought the most beautiful of her gold rings to the Klein Jewelry Store. She had a plan. She had thought it out carefully as she lay awake, night after night, in the large feather bed beside her husband. As she untied the handkerchief in which she hid the ring, she said:

"I want you should put a new stone in for me."

Both Mr. and Mrs. Klein came forward, smiling, and examined the gold ring carefully. Mrs. Klein leaned over the counter and there was a flicker of excitement in her eyes.

"What kind stone do you want? A diamond—maybe?"

Mrs. Strassburg fanned her face with the end of her silk scarf.

"Ya—the best stone you got. Something fine—something extra fine!"

Mrs. Klein slipped the ring on her short fat finger. It stuck on the first joint. She looked eagerly at Mrs. Strassburg.

"Nu, tell me—for what you want this ring—such a beautiful ring?" She pulled the ring off and laid it gently on the counter.

"You have such beautiful rings! My Dora loves so much your rings. She always says to me—Mrs. Strassburg has such beautiful rings. Ya, my Dora always says that to me."

Mrs. Klein paused and watched the expression on Mrs. Strassburg's face. Mrs. Klein was shrewd. She said things innocently, but she didn't mean them that way.

But she didn't fool Mrs. Strassburg. Mrs. Strassburg understood just what Mrs. Klein meant, and she was pleased. She wanted Dora for Karl as much as Mrs. Klein wanted Karl for Dora. If her son married Dora he would be rich all his life. He would own a fine house, and a car, and have money in the bank. Dora would bring him a fine dowry. She would give him something on which to build his life.

At first Mrs. Strassburg had held herself aloof whenever the Kleins had insinuated that they wanted Karl for Dora. She had seemed a little contemptuous, a little proud. After all, a mother doesn't have to hurry her son to get married. But a daughter must get married. She must never be left on the hands of her parents.

But no matter how aloof she had been, she had always kept in mind that Dora was for Karl.

However, one never knew what life held. So she played her game cleverly. She went to the Klein house often and accepted invitations for dinner and sat at the table loaded with heavy diamonds—and smiled and laughed and planned for Karl.

The Kleins had never lost sight of her diamonds. They were heavy and solid in her gold rings, and she flipped her delicate hands often in their faces, and let them catch the beauty of her stones.

She was aware that Mrs. Klein looked at them often, and that Mrs. Klein was dreaming of the day when she would see those rings on Dora's fingers. Mrs. Strassburg knew all this. She used to lie awake all night and torment her husband with dreams she had woven for Karl. She used to talk to him for hours, telling and retelling him the plans for her strategy. She would get the Kleins, but they wouldn't know it. She would get the dowry, and they would be glad to give it. She would get half their fortune for Karl, and they wouldn't be aware of her cleverness.

She would talk far into the night, until her husband's eyes would close helplessly, and he would bury his head in the large pillow to keep out the sound of her voice.

But she talked on and on, hardly aware that he had fallen asleep and didn't hear her plans. But it didn't matter that he didn't hear them. He was no part of them. She controlled Karl's life. She controlled her husband's life. She controlled everything!

At first Karl was indifferent to his mother's hopes

for him. He didn't understand she was trying to dominate him as she dominated his father. He accepted Dora casually. She was pretty and soft and she laughed a great deal. He liked to take her out, because she always wore the finest clothes. But he had never thought of marriage until his mother had insinuated that Dora would make him a good wife.

Karl laughed at first. Mrs. Strassburg was not discouraged. She talked to him always of Dora—Dora—and he always laughed.

His mother resented his laughter. It didn't fit in with her plans. One day she broke into sobs when he laughed. He was moved by her tears, and promised to do anything to make her happy.

She never forgot the power of her tears. She had used them often. She had always met with success until that night when Karl had left her in the store —that night when her sobs and her pleas had meant nothing to him—that night when he left her crushing the ring she had taken from his pocket, and gone to Ruby.

A flush of anger colored her face when she thought of that girl who had brought such tragedy into her life. She fingered the ring on the counter.

"Do you know to whom I am going to give this ring, Mrs. Klein?"

Mrs. Klein shrugged her shoulders and tried to look innocent.

"How should I know?"

Mrs. Strassburg leaned over the counter and whispered in Mrs. Klein's face:

"This ring is for the girl my Karl is going to marry. Maybe your Dora—who knows?"

She paused dramatically to see the expression in Mrs. Klein's face. Mrs. Klein's eyes twinkled with excitement, little beads of moisture stood on her upper lip.

"Ya! A lucky girl—a very happy girl. Such a wonderful ring!" She took it up and held it in her hand.

"We all wish for the happiness of our sons—and our daughters. They are little ones—and then soon, soon they get married."

She smiled through her crocodile tears. Mrs. Strassburg was unmoved. Mrs. Klein's tricks were not unlike her own.

CHAPTER XX

KARL resented his mother's interference in his life. She hadn't spoken to him since that night he had left her and gone to Ruby. He hadn't told Ruby about it. He didn't want her to know that his mother had chosen Dora for him.

He was afraid of losing Ruby, of having her slip out of his life as casually as she had slipped in. He needed Ruby. He wanted her more than he wanted anything else in the world. Ruby had never spoken to him about his mother, and he never knew whether she realized how his mother hated her.

Day after day, Mrs. Strassburg watched Karl in the store, and waited for him grimly until he came home at night. But she refused to speak to him. She only glanced at him with tragic eyes.

He couldn't endure her silence. He couldn't stand coming home every night and seeing that expression in her eyes as she rocked so silently in the chair. He couldn't stand going to the store every day and having her watch him. He hated that look because he knew he couldn't fight it.

Finally, he went to her.

"Don't be mad, ma—please!"

She smiled smugly. She had been waiting patiently for those words from him. She wanted him to beg her for her forgiveness—to break him—to make him come to her. And he had come. And she had remained cold as granite, and unforgiving.

Karl was miserable.

"Aren't you ever going to speak to me, ma?"

His dark, lustrous eyes were pleading. He felt so helpless in the power of her silence. At last she held out her beautiful, nervous hands to him:

"My Karl—my son!"

Then she broke down and wept. But her tears were not bitter. There were plentiful—and in her heart there was rejoicing. She would take Ruby out of his soul, and out of his life.

"My Karl—my son!"

He was relieved that his mother had spoken to him at last. No matter what she did he loved her. But he was also sad. He knew that her power to hurt him was great.

"I want you should be happy, Karl."

She smiled a beautiful smile, and at that moment she looked as she must have looked long ago when she twisted the heart of his father in her lovely hands.

"I know you do, ma."

She kissed him. "Karl, you will do everything to make me happy—ya?"

He didn't dare look at her. He knew what she was

going to ask him. She was going to ask him to give up Ruby. But he knew in his heart that he wouldn't give up Ruby, even if his mother closed her lips to him forever.

Mrs. Strassburg read his thoughts. They were written so clearly on his fine, brown face.

"You want to make me happy, Karl—ya?"

"Sure, I do, ma."

Mrs. Strassburg watched him shrewdly. She knew what there was in his heart. She knew him better than anyone else in the world. She knew what he expected her to ask, and she was determined not to ask it. Her strategy was greater than that. Instead, she asked:

"You will come with me this summer like always to the hotel up the river?"

He smiled gratefully. He had been so afraid that she would say something against Ruby.

"Sure!"

"It's no good only to work all the time—it's no good, Karl."

She was already planning how to run the store and go at the same time. Karl was wondering how he would be able to please his mother and yet see Ruby. But he didn't say anything more. He was too grateful for the new peace that had come to him since his mother had spoken to him at last.

Mrs. Strassburg was never more charming than

she was during those days when she and Karl were waiting for the summer. But he didn't know what she and Mrs. Klein were planning.

Mrs. Klein was making new dresses for Dora, and buying fine laces and silk. She was putting away expensive bolts of ribbons and yards of beautiful satin. She bought fine voiles and cottons, and had them made up in intriguing styles best fitted for Dora's figure. She had engaged the best dressmaker in town, and she had spent a fat sum. But it was all worth it. Mrs. Klein had made up her mind not to let the summer slip away without some profit.

Karl knew nothing about his mother's plans. He only knew that she didn't cry any more. She was placid and happy, and left him alone. Not once had she mentioned Ruby's name. She didn't mention Dora's name either, except when she wanted him to take Dora to some Jewish affair.

At first he would refuse. But when Mrs. Strassburg's eyes fastened on him beseechingly and large tears welled in them, he always relented.

He was afraid of her silence again. So he would take Dora, and meet Ruby afterwards. And he was glad his mother didn't know. He was pleasing her and pleasing himself, and it was easier that way.

But he wasn't happy. He hated meeting Ruby so secretly, and he was afraid that his mother would find out. He was afraid that someone would find out, and it nearly drove him insane.

After he had been with Dora for an evening, and listened to her chatter he was always more eager to be with Ruby than ever.

Later, in the store, he would feverishly tell Ruby of his love for her—his plans to marry her. He never had the courage to tell her about Dora. But he did tell her of the strange feeling of race the Jews had. He would tell her nervously, excitedly. She would listen to him.

He sometimes wondered if she understood. But one touch of her hand in his hair and it didn't matter whether she understood or not. She was his—and he was sure nobody in the whole world knew of their romance.

But, now, Carrie knew. And Nicki knew. And Mrs. Strassburg knew. Carrie had talked contemptuously about it, trying to infuriate Ruby. She sometimes did infuriate her, and then Carrie's heart pounded with fear. She was always afraid that Ruby would strike her. But Ruby never did.

Nicki said nothing. He only looked at Ruby with sultry eyes. But he was not discouraged. He waited grimly and smiled, often and sweetly, and stayed with Carrie at night, and dreamed of Ruby.

And Mrs. Strassburg dreamed of her, too. She saw Ruby's white face crushed and broken like the ring. And Mrs. Strassburg smiled in her sleep.

CHAPTER XXI

THE summer came at last. Mrs. Strassburg changed all the furniture in the window of the store, gave her husband detailed orders, polished her diamonds, and then in all her glory started for the hotel up the river.

Her husband was glad to see her leave. He was grateful for the quiet days and nights that would come to him.

She was reluctant to leave him at the same time that she was glad to go. She knew she would miss the enjoyment of her sharp words that she flung at him. She knew that she was going to miss those busy nights at the store, when she took the business in her own hands, and left her husband helpless and crushed. She enjoyed those looks of contempt she threw at him. They gave her a feeling of greatness. But she knew she must sacrifice this to go with Karl to the hotel up the river.

She talked it over with her husband a thousand times. But she didn't need his consent. Her plans had been made a long time ago, and nothing in the world could stop her. She loved intrigue and trickery.

Karl didn't tell Ruby he was going away. He knew

he could drive back into town every night to see her
—and his mother would never know. Besides, it was
a chance to get away from the store. He was getting
to hate that store—except at night when Ruby was
with him.

He used to like going to the hotel in the summer
with his mother. He used to look forward to it. All
the wealthy Jewish families went there. They had
such good times, and the nights were so long and full
of laughter.

He remembered the happy summers he had had
there with Dora and her sister, Mollie, and all their
friends. Dancing at night and row boat rides on the
river. He used to take Dora out on the moonlit river.
She was so gay and pretty, and her mouth was so
soft. He used to row his boat into the moon's bright
path. He and Dora used to stay out until it was slim
and pale.

Once when they were lying on the beach together
at midnight, Dora had dared him to go into the river.
She had giggled and run off into the pine grove and
started to take off her clothes. He wanted to follow
her, but she held up her dress in front of her, and
screamed:

"Don't look! Don't look!"

He promised he wouldn't look at her. He sat on
the sand and thought of her nudity. Then she ran
into the river. She wasn't nude at all. She wore a

brilliant yellow bathing suit, and she giggled nervously, pleased she had fooled him.

"Come on in—come on in!" She beckoned to him.

But he wouldn't go into the water after her. Instead he watched her swim and splash around on her
back. Was she swimming? He wondered. For Dora
had never wanted to learn to swim. He had tried to
teach her every summer, and she had let him put his
arms on her breasts and hold her up, and she had
laughed and splashed and pretended to be helpless.

He watched her that night from where he lay on
the sand. She called to him again. When he started to
take off his clothes and go into the water after her,
she laughed, taunting him, and swam around to the
other side of the shore.

That was the first time he knew that she could
really swim. It amused him. He was beginning to
understand Dora had been pretending to be afraid
of the water. She wanted him to feel he was very
strong. Strange how much Dora was like his mother.
They both were full of tricks.

So he sat on the sand instead of going after Dora,
and waited for her to swim back to him. He lit a
cigarette and blew the smoke through his nose and
watched the moon.

He sat there a long time. But she didn't come back.
At last he called her name. She didn't answer. He ran
through the pine grove around the bend of the shore.

Her clothes were gone. Her yellow bathing suit was hanging on a bush.

She had fooled him again. So he went back to the hotel and passed her on the porch without speaking. She was swinging in the hammock, completely dressed.

She called to him, but he passed her by. Then she reached back and caught his hand and pulled him down on the hammock beside her, and laughed like a little girl. She put her arms around his neck and begged him to forgive her. She told him she had run away because she was afraid.

She dropped her eyes when she said that. Karl got a little red. They remained together swinging on the dark porch. He tried to kiss her. She giggled and ran away. He went after her and pinned her against a tree. Her face was flushed and her breath was coming quickly. She watched him shrewdly, and waited for him to kiss her.

When he took her in his arms, she sighed with relief. She had planned the whole evening, and it had ended exactly as she wanted.

Later that night, she tossed on her bed, and dreamed of Karl, and made up her mind to make him her husband.

But he didn't know that. He only knew that she was prettier than any other Jewish girl, and that he liked to kiss her.

CHAPTER XXII

KARL had gone with Dora a whole summer. She had been his girl. Everybody in his crowd knew that Karl Strassburg was going with Dora Klein. It was no secret.

But all that happened before he met Ruby. The whole world had changed for him since he met Ruby. He didn't want Dora any more.

All through the long, dusty ride to the hotel on the river, he thought of Ruby and wondered how soon he could get away from his mother and ride back to her—back over sixty miles to town.

Dora was sitting on the porch, dressed in a new flowered chiffon dress when he arrived with his mother. She waved to them, kissed Mrs. Strassburg. Then she held out her hand to Karl.

"Hello, Karl—staying for the summer?"

Mrs. Strassburg was pleased with Dora's appearance. She was relying on Dora—counting on her to save Karl. She embraced Dora tenderly.

"Is mamma here, too, Dora?"

Mrs. Strassburg asked this innocently. She already knew that Mrs. Klein had been at the hotel two days before they arrived. It was planned that way. Dora understood that Mrs. Strassburg knew.

"Yes. Mollie's here, too. Papa's coming over Sunday."

"A lot of people here already, Doraleh?"

"The hotel's full—everybody in town is staying. The Ginsbergs got the big room with the bay window—and the Rubins took the two small rooms on the first floor—and Tessie Gluck and her father took the best rooms in the place—the ones mamma wanted. Mamma was so mad!"

Mrs. Strassburg raised her eyes in horror. Tessie Gluck and her father had no right to the best rooms —they were ordered special for the Kleins.

"So what happened? You didn't get the rooms?"

"Yes, after an argument. Mamma told that Tessie something—and was that Tessie fresh! Now they got the two rooms in back—the ones the Levines had last year."

"Ya—ya—I know. Well, I hope they got good food like they had last year."

Dora laughed. "I gained too much last year. I want to keep thin."

Mrs. Strassburg looked horrified.

"Never mind to get thin. It's no good! I like better you should eat and be healthy."

Dora blushed and smoothed down the frills on her new chiffon dress. She turned to Karl:

"I haven't seen you for a long time, Karl. What've

you been doing?" Her eyes flashed and the color rose to her face.

Mrs. Strassburg felt that Dora was making the right attack, and she patted her cheek and walked off.

Karl stood awkwardly, not knowing what to say to Dora. He felt strained in her presence. He wondered, now, as he looked at her, how he had ever thrilled to the taste of her mouth.

"Aren't you glad to see me, Karl?"

Her heart was pounding like a hammer. She sensed his apathy, and it wounded her deeply.

"Sure, I am."

But Dora could see that he didn't mean what he said. But somehow she didn't care. It was enough for her that he said it. It gave her courage.

"You don't know how happy I am to know that. I thought you were forgetting me."

Her voice trembled as she went on: "I suppose I'm silly—but that's because I'm so happy, I guess." She looked at him innocently, as if she didn't mean to flatter him. She wanted him to think that she was guileless and childlike.

"Let's go up to the hotel. It's silly standing here." She linked her arm through his.

Mrs. Strassburg watched them from the window. So did Mrs. Klein. And Dora looked up and waved, and tightened her clasp on Karl's arm.

"We'll have another good summer, Karl. There'll be lots of fun here. It will be wonderful—just wonderful! They got a new orchestra—and lots of new boats—and they've built an open air pavilion."

She hesitated a moment.

"There's a big dance tonight, Karl."

"Is there?"

"Everybody's going—all the old crowd. You will go, too—won't you?"

"Are you going, Dora?"

She fluttered a handkerchief in his face. It was drenched in Oriental perfume.

"Yes—if you'll be there! I don't care to dance with the other fellows. They—they don't count any more with me."

Then she fled like a frightened little girl.

He watched her go up the steps to the hotel. She stopped, blew him a kiss.

"See you tonight, Karl!"

Then she disappeared.

He never saw her again that day. He drove back to town—and stayed until morning. He had missed the dance completely.

Chapter XXIII

THE evening of the dance, as Dora waited for Karl she was conscious of her prettiness. She lifted her new dress carefully, and sat down on the swing, and looked a long time at her silver slippers. They were beautiful and very new, and they burned her feet a great deal. They were not meant for comfort. They were bought for beauty. She didn't intend to dance all evening. She had built her hopes on the moonlit river. There, in the darkness, she would make herself irresistible to Karl.

She saw everybody leave the hotel. They walked in a crowd, arm in arm, and laughed hilariously. But Dora sat alone. She wanted to be aloof and indifferent. Their conversation didn't interest her at all. She was thinking of Karl and what she would say to him.

She had rehearsed it all in her room. She would be more attractive tonight than she had ever been before. She smiled smugly to herself, and turned out the light on the porch and sat in the darkness. She was very effective in the darkness. She had found that out long ago.

Soon she heard the music. The dance had begun.

She looked out anxiously toward the pavilion and wondered if all the boys missed her. She was the best dancer in the crowd.

But she didn't care about anyone tonight. She could only think of Karl and what marriage to him would mean. He was the most important young man in the town. Besides, he was attractive and intense, and made you feel so warm and strange when he kissed you.

She tapped her silver slipper impatiently against the railing of the verandah, and listened unwillingly to the music. She had missed the first two dances.

"Doraleh! You look so beautiful tonight—like a doll!"

Mrs. Klein had come out on the porch to inhale the fresh air. She sat close to her daughter.

"Wait till Karl sees you—wait, Doraleh!"

Dora smiled. She was so pleased with her perfection.

"You look like a doll—such a beautiful doll!"

Mrs. Klein was very proud of her offspring. Dora, especially, was her joy—her life. Dora was the one who would make a profitable marriage. Mollie was good and kind, but Dora was like money in the bank.

"Mrs. Strassburg can be proud she'll get such a daughter like you."

Dora laughed softly. It was a pleasant thought, being Mrs. Strassburg's daughter. It meant she would inherit the diamonds, the business and Mrs. Strassburg's son. She wanted the son, and she wanted the diamonds. She could show them both off proudly.

"The Strassburgs got a good business now—haven't they, mamma? I heard papa say they were worth quite a lot."

Dora was already building her future. She wanted it to be substantial and strong.

"Sure, they got money. Papa wouldn't let you marry without first he knows how much they got. He don't want his Doraleh shouldn't have everything in the world. Papa's good, believe me, Doraleh —there ain't another man so good like papa."

"I know papa's good—and I know he wants me to have everything."

"Sure! Papa likes his children. Only for Mollie it's different. She ain't so pretty like you—she ain't got such good eyes. But if Mollie marries papa will give him plenty, too. Papa don't have to give so much with you, Doraleh."

Mrs. Klein beamed on her daughter.

"Believe me, the Strassburgs should thank God they found such a girl like you!"

"Sure, they should, mamma. After all, papa's a rich man. He'll give me a good send-off."

"Ya—ya, Doraleh. Papa's worked a whole life, his daughters should have everything. Papa ain't so well either."

"Poor papa, he shouldn't eat such heavy food."

"Doraleh—who can tell papa anything! He's got such a temper. When I tell him something, he falls on me with such words!"

"I know, mamma. But papa's good. He doesn't mean what he says."

"Ya, Doraleh, papa's good—papa's good!"

Mrs. Klein rocked back and forth on the swing, her short, fat legs hardly touching the floor.

Dora looked out toward the pavilion nervously.

"Mamma, I wish Karl would come. I'm getting so tired waiting."

"He'll come, Doraleh—you shouldn't worry."

"Mamma, I love you—I love papa—you're both so good to me. I won't forget you when I'm married. I'll come over to the house every day. I'll be there for dinner every night. I won't forget you."

Mrs. Klein started to cry a little softly. She loved Dora more than anything in her life. It would be difficult to give her up to Mrs. Strassburg.

"Mrs. Strassburg will see you more than me. You'll live with her in that big house. You'll be with her every day."

Dora tossed her dark curls defiantly.

"Not me, mamma. She won't be able to tell me what to do." She paused and whispered fiercely: "Mamma, sometimes I don't like Mrs. Strassburg!"

Mrs. Klein dried her eyes quickly.

"Sh!—Sh! Doraleh, you must like her—you shouldn't say that!"

"But I can't help it, mamma. She wants everyone to do what she says. She won't make me do what she wants. Not me!"

Mrs. Klein gripped her daughter's arm tightly.

"Doraleh, Mrs. Strassburg brought to the store a beautiful ring. Papa put in a big stone."

Dora held her breath a moment. Then she leaned forward eagerly.

"For me, mamma?"

Mrs. Klein smiled a little mysteriously.

"Who knows?"

"What kind of a stone? A diamond, mamma?"

"Ya—ya, Doraleh—a diamond."

"Is it bigger than Birdie Schmidt's—is it?"

"Ya—ya, Doraleh—a beautiful ring."

"What kind of a ring? Was it platinum?"

"No, no—gold."

The eagerness faded from Dora's face.

"I don't want a gold ring! I want platinum! Gold's old fashioned. All the girls got platinum!"

Her voice rose in protest. Her mother looked around with frightened eyes. She was afraid Mrs. Strassburg might hear Dora.

"Sh—sh! I tell you, it's a beautiful ring!"

"I don't like gold!"

"So—after you're married, you'll change it to

platinum."

"That's what I'll do."

They sat together in the swing, talking in low voices about Dora's future with Karl. Mollie rushed up the steps with one of the boys, flushed and happy.

"Dora, come on down! Everybody's dancing!"

"I'm waiting for Karl." Dora was resentful.

"But it's late! That was the fifth dance!"

"I'm sorry, Mollie. You go with Sam. I won't go without Karl."

The music started again. She heard Mollie's laugh and Sam's voice as they disappeared in the darkness. She became a little frightened. It was getting late. Suppose Karl wasn't coming at all—suppose he had left her here alone and gone off somewhere with someone else?

"Mamma, maybe Karl won't come tonight!"

She said the words over and over, and each time she said them her voice grew more frantic. She clutched her mother's arm. Mrs. Klein was frightened, too. After all, it was late, and Karl had not yet appeared. Dora started to cry. They were tears of anger.

"Mamma, something's happened!"

"No, Doraleh—Karl wouldn't do such a thing."

"Yes, he would—he would! It's that blond he's crazy about! He's gone to her, mamma!"

"No, Doraleh. Mrs. Strassburg told me he don't

want that girl no more."

"She knows a fat lot!"

"Sh—Doraleh!"

"He's gone off with her tonight! I know—I know!"

Mrs. Klein's heart was aching for her daughter. How could Karl go off like this and leave Dora so alone, so unhappy!

The moon was getting pale, and the night was coming in darker and heavier than before. Mother and daughter sat on together, pretending to listen to the music.

It was beautiful music, and Dora wanted to dance tonight. It was a night amorous and balmy. It was a night meant for sitting on the shore after a long, languid dance and cooling your blood in the moonlight and feeling the cool sand on your feet.

Mollie came running back to the verandah again.

"Didn't Karl come yet?"

"Go back, Mollie. Never mind Dora."

But Mollie hesitated. "Everybody's been asking for Dora and Karl."

Mrs. Klein flashed Mollie a bitter look.

"Go back, dummy what you are—don't say nothing!"

"Will I tell them she's still waiting for Karl?"

Dora jumped up quickly.

"Don't you dare tell them that! Don't you dare!"

Mollie backed away from her sister. Her little eyes flickered helplessly behind her thick glasses.

"I didn't mean anything, Dora—honest! Don't get mad!"

But Dora's pride had been hurt. She screamed at the bewildered Mollie.

Mrs. Klein cracked her hands together. She was terrified that Dora would be heard. Dora would spoil everything. Dora would ruin the chances for her marriage with her ugly temper.

"Doraleh—you should be quiet!"

Dora turned on her mother violently. The placid prettiness of her was gone entirely.

"I won't be quiet! I won't! I'll fix Karl! I'll do something to him to make him suffer like I've suffered! You wait and see what I'll do!"

She broke down into heavy, passionate sobs.

Mollie stood by silently, and Mrs. Klein cracked her hands together. She didn't know what else to do.

"Doraleh, maybe he couldn't help it! Something, maybe, happened!"

Dora stamped her silver slippers in fury.

"What do you mean, he couldn't help it? He could help it! He did it on purpose! I'll fix him! Wait and see—I'll fix him!"

She screamed the words in anguish, and then glared at Mollie resentfully.

Mollie touched Dora timidly. "Come down, Dora,

you can have a good time. It's not too late."

But Dora pushed her roughly away. She didn't want Mollie's sympathy.

"Leave me alone! You needn't try to be nice to me just because Karl didn't show up. I don't need your sympathy!"

With a little secret gesture, Mrs. Klein indicated to Mollie to return to the pavilion. Dora was standing with her hand on her heart.

"I got a pain, too, Doraleh." Mrs. Klein looked upon her pretty daughter with sad eyes.

After a few moments, Dora drew herself up proudly and narrowed her eyes. They were red and swollen.

"I'll show him! I'll show him, all right!"

She rushed into the hotel, and up to her room. Mrs. Klein was left alone on the porch. She had never been so miserable as she was tonight.

When Dora appeared on the porch again, the swollen look had gone from her eyes. She was pink and lovely again.

"I'm going anyway, mamma. I'll have a good time."

"Sure—Doraleh—sure! A good time—that's what you should have!"

Mrs. Klein was relieved.

"Mamma, don't you dare to tell those cronies of yours what Karl did to me. I don't want anyone in this place to know."

Mrs. Klein promised faithfully, and Dora ran down to the pavilion. She wondered what Mrs. Strassburg would say if she knew how Karl had wounded Dora.

Chapter XXIV

The next morning Mrs. Klein went to see Mrs. Strassburg. She had thought about it all night. She was a good mother. Dora's happiness was more important to her than anything else in the world—and that happiness depended upon a substantial marriage. And that marriage depended on Mrs. Strassburg.

Mrs. Klein had figured it out carefully. It had taken a long time to get it smooth and perfect in her head. She was not a brilliant woman. She was full of tricks but not a strategist like Mrs. Strassburg.

She put on her golden chain and pinned her large watch to her bosom and walked timidly to Mrs. Strassburg's room. She was afraid that Dora would catch her. She had promised her daughter not to tell anyone what Karl had done. But she had to tell Mrs. Strassburg. She could not bear to think that Dora's wound would go unpunished.

Mrs. Strassburg was counting her diamonds when Mrs. Klein appeared in the room. She was wrapped in her husband's bathrobe, and her face was flushed as she picked up each ring from the pile in her lap and dropped it back in the little chamois bag.

Mrs. Klein watched her curiously. The diamonds were good to look upon. They made it clearer to her how important it was to save Karl and place him safely in Dora's hands.

She prepared herself by dropping comfortably in a large chair and folding her hands across her stomach. She sighed and all the time watched the rings drop from Mrs. Strassburg's fingers.

"Ah, Mrs. Strassburg—I got a heart full this morning."

Mrs. Strassburg looked up at her. Then she dropped the last ring in her bag and pulled the string tightly.

"So why you got a heart full? What's the matter?"

Mrs. Klein sighed mournfully.

"What's the matter? Believe me, I got plenty what's the matter!"

"You're sick? Your husband's sick—maybe?"

Mrs. Klein shook her head.

"No, thank God! But my Doraleh—my beautiful Doraleh cried all night!" Mrs. Klein almost broke down when she said those words.

"Doraleh's sick, Mrs. Klein?"

Mrs. Klein clasped and unclasped her hands.

"No, she ain't sick, but she's got a pain in the heart, Mrs. Strassburg—such a terrible pain in the heart! It's a whole story—such an upset, I can't tell you—"

Mrs. Strassburg could hardly stand the suspense. Something had happened last night and she didn't know anything about it. She leaned forward excitedly.

Mrs. Klein took a deep breath and looked very sad. She could hardly go on with the story.

Mrs. Strassburg was burning with curiosity, and her eyes shone. She suddenly looked very wise, and then she spoke in a quick excited tone:

"I'm telling you, Mrs. Klein—I had a feeling something wasn't so good. I didn't sleep the whole night myself."

Mrs. Strassburg lied magnificently, and she flung out her beautiful hands dramatically. Mrs. Klein smiled a gentle smile. She believed that Mrs. Strassburg's sleep had been disturbed because Dora was unhappy. Things like that happened in life when there was a great love. She was sure of great love and understanding between Mrs. Strassburg and Dora. Maybe Dora didn't like Mrs. Strassburg so much— but Mrs. Strassburg loved Dora, and that was important.

"Believe me, Mrs. Strassburg, you love my Dora-leh."

"Ya—ya—I love her."

"My Doraleh loves you, Mrs. Strassburg. Ya, she loves you like a real mother."

Mrs. Strassburg was pleased. She could already see

Dora the wife of Karl, bringing him a large part of the Klein money.

"I'm so happy, Mrs. Klein, that your Doraleh loves me." She wiped a tear from the corner of her eye.

Mrs. Klein was very pleased that Mrs. Strassburg was so touched by Dora's affection for her. It was a beautiful and comforting thing. She folded her hands and started to tell the story.

"You know, Mrs. Strassburg, what a beautiful new dress my Dora had last night. You know, Mrs. Strassburg, she looked like a regular doll."

Mrs. Strassburg nodded her head. She felt very kindly toward Mrs. Klein this morning.

"Your Dora is a regular beauty."

Mrs. Klein clucked her lips, a sharp light flashed through her little eyes.

"So what's the matter with your Karl? Why should he do such a thing to her?"

Mrs. Strassburg's mouth dropped open.

"What did he do?" A look of fear shot through her eyes.

"He said he wanted Doraleh should go with him to the dance. My Doraleh has so many boys, I tell you, Mrs. Strassburg—everyone they was so excited to take her. But, you know, after all, Doraleh didn't see Karl for so long—so she told him she liked better to go with him."

"So—so?"

"So, she gets dressed in her new dress—and sits on the porch—and waits for him."

"So—so?"

"So, she waits—and waits—and he doesn't come."

"So—so?"

"So—nothing! Doraleh was so ashamed. After all, Mrs. Strassburg, I'm proud of my Dora. She don't need to wait for no boy. She got maybe a million already."

Mrs. Strassburg was stunned. She had thought Karl had gone to the dance with Dora. He told her he would go. She had felt so triumphant because she thought she had kept him away from Ruby.

Karl had fooled her, and she thought she had fooled him. All last night she had played whist with the ladies in her room, and she had flipped her cards in high spirits, and she had won. And all the time Karl was somewhere with Ruby while Dora was on the porch, crying bitterly.

Mrs. Strassburg wet her dry lips with her tongue, and folded her hands against her heart.

"Ach—ach, Mrs. Klein. If only I knew that! If only I knew that last night!"

Mrs. Klein set her mouth. She looked curiously like Dora when she was hurt.

"It's a shame and disgrace that Karl should do such a thing. If he wants to go with that blond girl

—nu, so good!—but he don't have to hurt my Dora-leh. He don't have to do that!"

She said these words so easily, as if it didn't matter whether Karl wanted Dora or not. But she glanced at Mrs. Strassburg furtively. She was only pretending not to care. She did care. She would have struck down Ruby and crushed her beautiful face and felt no pity if it would have brought happiness to Dora. She continued:

"Believe me, any boy what gets my Dora is lucky. But Karl—he don't want something good like her."

Mrs. Klein hesitated. She did it purposely. It was somehow sinking through her head that she was playing a brilliant game with Mrs. Strassburg.

"He's got such a good—such a wonderful mother like you."

Mrs. Strassburg swayed back and forth on the bed, and beat her breast in heavy, even strokes. But she said nothing—nothing.

Mrs. Klein was getting impatient. She wanted something to bring back to Dora. She wanted a fragile word of hope, a bitter expression of hate, something—something for her daughter. She couldn't interpret Mrs. Strassburg's silence very well. It was too deep, too profound for her more sluggish brain. She blinked her eyes nervously and twisted her golden chain, and drew in her little head between her fat shoulders, and waited for Mrs. Strassburg to speak.

Mrs. Strassburg spoke, at last, in a bitter voice.

"You shouldn't say another thing. You should go back to Doraleh. Forget what Karl did."

Mrs. Klein twisted in her chair. She was disappointed in Mrs. Strassburg's answer. It was so calm, so completely without dramatics. She pushed her little head forward, and her eyes were blurred with unhappy tears.

"My Doraleh cried a whole night!"

Mrs. Strassburg nodded her head. There was still that strange shining look in her eyes.

"Mrs. Klein, with goodness one gets everything. With harsh words one gets nothing. I won't say a bad word to Karl. I will be so nice—so sweet—so good to him."

Mrs. Klein was beginning to understand Mrs. Strassburg's strategy.

"What a wonderful woman you are, Mrs. Strassburg! What a wonderful woman!"

Mrs. Strassburg pulled her husband's bathrobe around her magnificently. Her vanity was great, and her shrewdness was something remarkable. She knew she was a wonderful woman. She waved her finger back and forth in Mrs. Klein's face.

"I made a rich man from my husband. I made a big store from nothing. I will do with Karl like I want—not like he wants. I brought him to this hotel for something—and believe me, Mrs. Klein, my Karl will only marry a Jewish girl. You hear me—a Jewish girl!"

Mrs. Klein took hold of Mrs. Strassburg's beautiful hands. "You are a wonderful woman—a wonderful woman!"

"You will see, Mrs. Klein, what I can do—you will see—you will see!"

"Ya—ya, Mrs. Strassburg! And my Doraleh—how she loves you!"

She went from Mrs. Strassburg's room and left her clutching her bag of diamonds—those diamonds that would some day glisten so brilliantly on Dora's little hands.

Chapter XXV

FOR two weeks after the dance at the summer hotel, Ruby didn't see Karl. She couldn't understand the reason. Her heart ached so that she finally decided to pass his store.

She put on her red shoes and combed out her hair. She went out past the Empire Hotel, and then down the street, and stopped in front of the Strassburg Furniture Store. She pressed her face against the window.

Karl was not there, but his father was. He saw her and motioned her away. He looked after her and shrugged his shoulders, sighed deeply, and shook his head. He was glad Karl was with his mother in the hotel up the river.

There was a pain in Ruby's flesh. She was trying to figure out what was the matter with Karl. He had left her one night when the fog covered the window panes of the store, and the lamps had been dimmed in the streets.

That was the night of the dance at the hotel when he had disappointed Dora.

Ruby remembered all their conversation that night.

"I don't care what happens to my mother," he told her.

"She don't like me."

"That isn't it, Ruby. Jews are funny about certain things—that's all."

"I know—Carrie told me that."

"What does she know?"

"She went with a Jew once."

"They aren't all alike, Ruby."

"All Jews stick together."

"Who told you that?"

"Carrie. She knows. She found that out with Maxie."

"Who was Maxie?"

"He was rich—he gave her a locket."

"I gave you a ring—but you wouldn't wear it."

"You ain't like Maxie."

"You're not like anyone else in the world."

"I ain't a Jew, though."

"What difference does that make? I love you just the same."

"Your mother hates me."

"My mother doesn't understand a lot of things."

"She don't know about tonight?"

"She thinks I'm at the hotel."

"She'd die if she knew you was here."

"Maybe—but what do I care?"

"I don't care about your mother, either."

"I don't care about anyone but you, Ruby. You believe that—don't you?"

It had been almost daylight when he drove back to the hotel up the river. He promised to come back the next night. He promised never to let her slip out of his life. She listened quietly as they drove through the silent night into the fog.

He dropped her at the hat shop, held her hand to his heart, then turned his car and rode away.

She stood in the fog with her hair clinging to her face, and clutching the heart-shaped box of candy he had brought her.

Then she unlocked the door and went inside.

She slept the whole next day, and then scrubbed her body with soap at night, and rubbed perfume under her arms, and into her hair, and waited for him to ride back to town.

But he didn't return again. Nothing remained of him but the heart-shaped box of candy.

CHAPTER XXVI

THE days dragged for Ruby. Every day, she walked past the Strassburg Furniture Store, but only Karl's father was there. She tried to avoid Nicki, passing his store quickly so that he wouldn't stop her. But, with Karl gone, Nicki gave Ruby no peace. At every possible moment he waylaid her. He stood before her, spreading his arms and wouldn't let her pass.

"Hello, Ruby."

She stepped away from him, threw back her head, and pushed out her lip defiantly.

"Get out of my way, you big wop!"

"What for you look so mad at Nicki?"

Her defiance did not seem to bother him.

"You look pretty nice today. Pretty shoes—pretty dress—I like pretty girl." He took her by the arm, but gently.

"Let go my arm!"

"Don't be mad at Nicki all the time." He smiled.

She pulled her arm away from him.

"Go away from me, you big wop!"

Nicki continued to smile. "But you like me sometimes—when I sing good songs—eh, Ruby?"

"You better leave me alone—see!"

"I never leave you alone, baby." But he stepped aside and let her pass.

"I let you go this time, baby—but some time you want Nicki. He got good heart, too—plenty money —big business. Nicki's all right, you betcha life— Nicki one good fella!"

"Go tell it to Carrie!" And she was gone.

Later he came to the hat shop. Carrie wasn't at home. Ruby was alone, playing her records over and over. She was thinking of Karl.

"Why you so alone, baby?"

"I ain't alone. Got music—ain't I?"

"Music all right sometimes—not when you alone."

"I like bein' alone."

"What's the matter with this boy? Why he let you sit here when it's such a good night—such a beautiful night!" His smile seemed painted, like it didn't go with the amorous look of longing in his eyes.

"You no like I tell you about that fellow—eh?"

He spoke kindly, but she hated the sweetness of his words. She knew his soft treachery and was afraid of it.

She played the victrola again. He watched her silently. Her whiteness and her vicious hate of him fascinated him. He had waited such a long time for Ruby. He had waited and planned and dreamed of her beauty. He licked his lips and the cords stood out on his neck as he struggled to keep his hands from her.

She leaned back on the chair and swayed to the music as if he were not there.

"You like nice songs—eh?"

She didn't answer. She was trying to hum the piece under her breath. Nicki listened for a moment. There was a warm, husky quality to her voice.

"Someday, you be a big singer—eh?"

She looked at him curiously, and the song died in her throat. But the tin horn of the victrola carried it on.

"Someday, you be a big singer all right—Nicki know that."

Ruby was indifferent to his praise. She selected another record and let it play over and over. All the time she thought of Karl.

The days were so dull without him. The nights were so long without him. Nothing to do. Nothing to say. Just sit in back of a dirty hat shop and feel the liquid eyes of a Greek fastened on you.

She lit the other lamps in the parlor. It was getting late. Another night was on its way.

Nicki saw the thin line of pain between her brows. It marred the smoothness of her skin. He saw the distant, cloudy look in her eyes.

"He no come tonight, Ruby. He got other girl."

Her throat quivered at his taunt.

"You don't like that Nicki tell you the truth."

"Go back to your store, Nick!"

"I take you back to my store with me. I have nice new records—Caruso—Galli Curci—Melba. You like these, baby. Sing very good."

The fragile beauty of her was more potent to him tonight than ever before.

"Baby, you come into my store, I play for you Caruso."

"Who's he?"

"He's a wop, Ruby—he sing so wonderful like a bird. Come—I show you."

She went because she wanted to hear Caruso.

Nicki brought out his jug of wine and two glasses, and the records he promised to play for her. He showed her the name—Caruso. Then he poured her a glass of wine.

"Drink—make you feel better, Ruby—happy."

She picked up the record with the name Caruso.

"Play this."

"Sure, sure, Ruby—but first you drink. Then you will be warm—you will smile—you will be nice to Nicki."

She drank the wine quickly, then held out the record to him. He put it on the machine, turned the handle and adjusted the tin horn. The disk turned, and then there burst forth a magnificent, rich voice. Ruby had never heard such a voice before. It was something magic—something throbbing with beauty.

She couldn't speak, she could only try to understand the flawless perfection of this golden voice. She liked the song, too. And he sang in a strange language. It must be Italian, because Caruso was Italian.

Nicki could see she was completely under the spell of the singer.

"He sing of love—this Caruso."

She nodded her head slowly.

"He sing of a man who love a girl—but she no love him. She love someone else—maybe a big man who got plenty money."

Caruso's voice was rising in a crescendo of sorrow. Nicki's voice sobbed, too.

"Hear, Ruby! Hear how he cry for that girl!"

The song ended. The golden voice was gone, but the magic of it remained.

"Play it again, Nick—play it again!"

He played it over and over for her. She never grew weary of the song. And Nicki played it for her gratefully. He loved music, too. But he loved more the belief that Ruby was forgetting Karl.

It was long after midnight when Karl suddenly appeared at the fruit store. Nicki looked up and saw him. He stumbled to his feet, and wiped the wine from his mouth. Karl had spoiled his evening.

"Get out of here! You hear me? Get out of here!"

He turned to Carrie.

"Why you bring him here?"

Carrie was white with fear. "Just came in from Georgia's—and he rings the bell and asks for Ruby. I heard the music and thought maybe she was here."

Karl looked at Ruby. She didn't seem to understand that he had come to her at last. She smiled strangely, but she didn't move. Karl didn't know she was still under the spell of the music—and the wine. Then he took her hand. She looked at him vaguely.

Nicki lunged toward Karl, and pushed the jug of wine from the table. It fell with a crash and broke into nothing.

"Get out before I kill you!"

He struck Karl viciously across the mouth. A line of blood pushed down his chin. Carrie screamed.

"Come on, Ruby." Karl spoke quietly.

Ruby took the record off the machine and went with him. She was beginning to understand that she had been waiting for him all evening.

Nicki was left alone with Carrie. He covered his face with his hands and cried out in anger. His longing for Ruby would never come to an end.

"Gee, what's the matter, Nick? What's the matter?"

"I kill her, Carrie! I no let her go 'round with him!"

She nodded her head slowly. "Sure, I know."

"I kill her, Carrie! I kill her!"

She nodded her head again. "Sure, Nick, you ought to."

But she couldn't keep up her pretense any longer. Her mouth suddenly wobbled. She broke down completely and went to him.

"She ain't goin' to take you from me, Nick—is she? She ain't goin' to do that!" She put her arm about his neck desperately.

He smiled grimly, and let her bury her head on his shoulder. It shut out her painted face. They sat together for a long time—Carrie sobbing and Nicki thinking—thinking—thinking of Ruby.

Chapter XXVII

KARL drove Ruby to a lonely place on the river. They went down to the edge of the water and sat on the sand.

"Ruby—Ruby—why were you with Nicki?"

He trembled when he thought of it, and there was pain still in the cut on his face.

"I was listenin' to Caruso."

"Caruso?"

"Nicki says he's the greatest singer in the world." She held out the record to him. He took it and threw it in the sand.

"I could kill that Greek!"

Her eyes darkened for a moment. "He thinks I can sing."

Karl buried his face in his hands, and Ruby thought he was crying. She was ashamed of tears, so she turned her head away and lay on the sand and shut her eyes and let the wind pass over her face and flutter in her hair. There was a sensuous silence between them. Finally, he lifted his face.

"Ruby, I wanted to come to you every night. I couldn't—it hasn't been my fault. I've tried to see you. I just couldn't—I couldn't!"

Ruby was very still. The magic beauty of Caruso was still in her heart. A few bars of the song hovered on her lips. She tried to catch its haunting quality again.

"If you only knew how miserable I've been, Ruby—how I've missed you!" He buried his face on her shoulder, and then he sobbed. They were terrible sobs, and he couldn't stop their agony.

Ruby passed her hand gently over his hair, and felt a great pity in her heart for him. She forgave him readily the unhappiness he had given her these two weeks.

"Karl—Karl—don't!"

His sobs were quieted. He raised his face.

"I wanted to see you so much—but my mother's been sick—she wanted me to stay with her. She wouldn't let me go. But tonight I couldn't stand it any longer. I had to see you! I love you more than anything in the world—more than anything!"

He began to feel at peace with Ruby. In these moments with her, he almost forgot the two weeks at the hotel with his mother and Dora. Those two weeks without Ruby! He couldn't understand now why he had remained with his mother. He had convinced himself he was justified in his duty to her. He hated that duty, and the power it had over him.

He held her in his arms. The night was coming in heavier than before, and the water looked dark and smooth and peaceful.

"What did you do all the time you didn't see me?"

"Nothin'."

"I want to take you away. I want to go to another place! I could open a store like my father's. I could make money. We'd get along."

"Where do you want to go?"

"Anywhere! Anywhere! It doesn't make any difference. I can't stand this any longer."

She said to him dully: "I know about that Jewish girl."

Her words startled Karl. He felt a little guilty about Dora. It was true that he had seen Dora every day, every night during those two weeks. But he couldn't help it. She was at the hotel. He couldn't escape Dora. And his mother—he knew it would bring her happiness if he married Dora. He also knew he would break her heart if he married Ruby.

And tonight he had Ruby. But earlier in the evening he had been with Dora. He was sitting alone on the hotel porch when she came to him.

"It's like old times, isn't it, Karl—you and me?" She sat down beside him. She laid her head on his shoulder.

"I'm so happy you're here, Karl."

He felt the curve of her bosom as she cuddled close to him. She was so gentle as she lay against his shoulder. But still he wanted to get away from her and go into town.

And then he didn't know how he got away from Dora, but he had come to town to Ruby. Desperate and miserable, he went to her house in the back of the hat shop. No one was there. Then Carrie arrived, and took him to Nicki's store.

"We're going to get married—I've made up my mind."

"Karl—Karl." She spoke his name in her husky voice that held a strange, passionate melody.

"Let's run away—tonight—tomorrow—let's get away from everyone!"

"Yes, Karl."

"I'll make money for both of us—we'll be all right—we'll be together."

They stayed together on the cold sand until the early morning. The record Nicki had given her with the strange Italian love song was buried in the sand.

CHAPTER XXVIII

WHEN the summer was over and the rich Jewish families went back to their homes, Karl returned to Ruby.

Nicki watched Karl fiercely, and Carrie began to hate Ruby with a jealous and terrible hate. She was sure Ruby was stealing Nicki from her.

Ruby did not know that Carrie hated her so bitterly. She hardly saw her aunt these days. She was happy with Karl.

Karl finally told his mother he was going to marry Ruby. It took great courage to make his decision, and once made, Karl appeared happier, calmer.

His mother screamed and gripped the table to keep herself from falling. His father was less dramatic:

"You mean you will bring her home to us—your wife?"

"I'm going to marry her, pa." Karl was firm.

His mother rocked back and forth in woe and cracked her hands and mumbled ancient prayers. "Karl, you should not do this. Karl—Karl!"

"But I love her, ma. I've tried to do what you wanted me to—marry Dora—but I don't love

Dora!"

His father tried to reason with him. Karl's mother was too broken to think coherently. "Karl, mamma has worked a whole life that you should marry a good girl."

"She is good, pa."

"But she is not one of us, Karl."

"What can I do about that! Is it her fault or my fault that she wasn't born of my religion!"

Mrs. Strassburg was still huddled pathetically and beating her chest. She was trying to ease her sorrow. But it was no use. She had been struck down by her tragedy, and in those few moments when Karl told her of his plans to marry Ruby, she had grown old and haggard. She spoke to her husband:

"Ben, what have we done to deserve such a punishment? What have we done?"

"Don't talk like that, ma—it's no punishment!"

She moaned and wailed. "You are out of my life, Karl! You have brought shame upon me!"

"No, ma—listen to me! You want me to be happy?"

"Ya, ya—I want you to be happy."

Karl turned to his father: "And you, pa, don't you understand I can never be happy married to Dora?"

His father spoke gently: "There are other girls beside Dora. But this one—this one! No, Karl, don't do this to mamma!"

Mrs. Strassburg's tears gave way to fury:

"You will never marry that girl! You'll see, Karl —while I live you'll never marry her!"

He flung back at her defiantly: "You can't stop me! No one can stop me!"

"Karl, Karl, listen to mamma." His father tried to make his son understand the great wrong he was committing.

But Karl would not listen. His fear for his mother —for his race—had disappeared.

"I've always listened to her and what has it got me? I'm through! I've told Ruby! She knows we'll have a struggle—she knows it won't be easy! But she's willing and I'm willing! I don't want Dora and all her money! And that's final!"

Mrs. Strassburg stood over her son magnificently. She was not the broken woman now. She was the great strategist. "She is very young, this girl—yes?"

He nodded his head.

"She has lived with bad people—I know. Didn't they all see you in a fight with that man—that man who lives in their house?"

"It's a lie, ma—a damn lie!"

"No, Karl—no! She could be put in a school—a school for such girls—ya!"

"You wouldn't do that, ma!"

She smiled tyrannically.

"She would stay there for a long time, Karl. I could do that! Your ma could do that!"

He was white. "You'll never do that! Never!"

She laughed and spit in defiance. "You should not speak with her more. You should keep away from that girl, Karl—you hear me! You should not speak with her more!"

Then Mrs. Strassburg walked from the store.

Karl was struck speechless. He beat his chest almost as his mother had done. Mr. Strassburg stood over him and stroked his rumpled hair.

"No, no, Karl—some day you will be happy that you did not marry this girl—for some day you will have children—good, strong children, and they will be of our race, my son."

Karl did not answer. He was stricken helpless before his mother's threat. His father continued kindly:

"Mamma is right, Karl. When you get to be an old man like me, and you have a son, too, then you will know what pain is in our hearts."

Again Ruby did not see Karl for many weeks. She was bewildered and lonely. Then she saw him on the street. He was with Dora. He hurried past Ruby as though he did not see her at all. But she knew he had seen her, and she stood in the street, and watched him until she couldn't see him any more.

So she went to the park every day and listened to the concerts, and sat alone until dark, and waited. He never came. But Dora came to the park, and she passed Ruby deliberately many times, and tossed her head in the air, and whispered to the other girls about Ruby. She could hear their laughter. It sounded cruel.

Then, after many weeks, she knew at last why he never came to her any more. Nicki showed her the clipping in the paper. It was on the second page. There was a picture of Dora, and a picture of Karl. They were going to be married. There was going to be a big wedding in the Synagogue.

Ruby dropped the paper on the floor, but she couldn't cry. Nicki was triumphant.

"Too bad, baby—he marry rich girl, I hear."

She stared at Nicki but she didn't see him. Her eyes were too blurred. Nicki was happy. He didn't hate Karl any more.

"Nice fella—good lookin'."

Ruby still sat silently.

"Listen, baby—Nicki never break your heart."

Then Carrie came in. She picked up the paper, laughed hilariously when she saw the pictures.

"That's Jews, all right—always stick together! Never mind, Ruby—he'll be comin' around one of these fine nights."

Carrie pulled out the locket that was hiding in the

folds of her massive breasts, and opened it, and looked at Maxie. He was still there, looking very young. Carrie sighed.

"A swell lookin' man Maxie was—nice curly hair —just like Karl."

Then Ruby spoke:

"Get out of here with Maxie!"

Carrie closed the locket, and put it back carefully.

"Get out both of you! Get out!"

Chapter XXIX

RUBY remained in her room in the back of the hat shop, day after day, night after night, alone, playing her victrola over and over. She never passed the Strassburg Furniture Store any more. But she thought of Karl all the time. He was gone now, forever. He hadn't fooled his mother, after all.

"Why you stay here all day—all night?" It was Nicki. He stood in the doorway.

She answered hoarsely: "I'm tired, Nick."

"Nicki, he no like see you look so sad."

But she didn't move, even to look up at him.

And then he told her what he had come to tell her: He told her that Karl was being married this night.

"He's happy tonight—why not you be happy, too? My friend give big party tonight—you go with me—we take Carrie."

"I don't feel like it, Nick."

But she went to the party. It was her way of destroying her image of Karl.

The party was very gay. It was given for Hazel, the girl with the hair like wool. She was giving up her business, now. She was going to marry Joe.

But Ruby couldn't endure the laughter and the wine, the loud, rude jokes of the men, the shrill voices of the women. While Nicki and Carrie were congratulating Hazel, she slipped through the crowd and went off.

She walked alone past the Synagogue where Karl's wedding was taking place. She sat on the stairs of a strange house across the way, and waited for the doors to open so she could see him.

She sat there a long time, and she heard the music that came from the wedding in the hall underneath the Synagogue. The Kleins had ordered the best musicians in town. They played well, songs that were sad and gay, full of brilliant Russian melody. It was the sort of music they always played at Jewish weddings for the older generation, who twisted their gold chains about their necks, and swayed to the Russian melodies, and dreamed of terrible days in Russia. They also played jazz. That was for the young people.

Then the doors opened. She knew that Karl belonged to Dora now. And Dora was happy. And Mrs. Strassburg with her beautiful hands and her brilliant eyes was happy, too.

Ruby got up and walked away. She didn't want to see Karl, after all. Besides she was afraid he would see her sitting on the steps of a strange house and waiting for him to appear. It made her feel ashamed.

Ruby hurried away and never turned around. She didn't see his dark face, or the ring on Dora's finger.

CHAPTER XXX

ONE day she met Karl on the street. He had just returned from his wedding trip. His face crimsoned when he saw her. Then he lingered in front of a store window, and pretended he hadn't seen her at all. But she knew he had seen her. He watched her through the window glass, and he saw her pass him by. He noticed that she looked beautifully white as always. When she turned the corner and out of sight, Karl hurried away and his hands were damp and cold and he felt miserable.

Day after day, Ruby walked aimlessly through the streets. She had no place to go. That's how she met Jed Hawkins.

Jed had just come in from Montreal with three trunks of fur coats. He carried the best line, and he was top salesman for the Phoenix Fur Company.

He was sitting in the window of the Empire Hotel looking over the town when Ruby went by. He flashed his diamond at her through the window, and he smiled. She looked at him coldly, and he pretended to be hurt. Then she smiled. She couldn't help it. His round face looked so silly when he pretended to be hurt, like a little boy whose hands had been slapped.

He asked her to model for him. And she did. She liked the feel of the fur and the heavy flowered linings. There was something luxurious in fur coats. She'd never had one on before.

Jed stayed in St. Marks for ten days, and sold his coats. One evening in a booth in a resturant, he said to Ruby:

"Got a big order in the next town—want to go with me, Gorgeous?"

Ruby smiled.

"You could model for me again—you're one swell little model."

She went with Jed. She wanted to get away from St. Marks for a while. It was getting on her nerves.

Carrie couldn't wait to tell Nicki that Ruby had gone off with a man who sold fur coats. She told him with a vicious smile. He smiled back at her, and his black hair shone under the orange lamp in the parlor. But Carrie didn't notice that his smile was fixed and ugly.

Ruby came back after four days, and she wore a long, gray squirrel coat that covered her like a blanket. She dangled a rose colored bag.

Ruby never saw Jed again, but she wore his fur coat all day. At night, she lay naked in her bed and pulled it over her and stroked the silky fur, and her eyes would soften. In the morning she wore the coat over her nightgown. She dragged it through the kitchen when she had her breakfast. She wore it defiantly when she walked down the street, wore it until the fur began to tear. Carrie loved the coat, too. She was getting very proud of Ruby.

CHAPTER XXXI

ONE afternoon, Karl saw her get into a long, cream-colored car. She made the man drive past the Strassburg Furniture Store. They drove past it many times as if they had suddenly gone mad. She liked the car. It was smooth as satin and had a musical horn.

Karl's heart stood still. "Ruby—Ruby—" he breathed her name. Then he dropped his hands to his sides. Dora had just come into the store.

Ruby came back to the hat shop that night, and showed Carrie all the beautiful things the man in the cream-colored car had bought her. She gave Carrie a pair of earrings with green stones. The man bought them for her in a pawn shop. He told her they belonged to a princess. The man had lied. But Ruby didn't care. She liked to see the eager light in her aunt's eyes.

"Gee, you're a good kid, Ruby."

Ruby left before Carrie could thank her again. She didn't want thanks. She hated Carrie. She only came home from her trips to flaunt her success in her aunt's face. She had never forgotten the morning her aunt told her she wouldn't have to go back to school. That was the morning Carrie and Nicki showed her the silk things they had taken from Red. She remembered that Nicki had said a girl could get nice things if she was smart. That's what Ruby was —smart!

Once she went off with a man who drew pictures. He worked for a corset concern. He drew Ruby's legs in thin, black lace stockings with blue satin garters over the knees. He was going to use the pictures for advertising the blue satin garters.

Ruby laughed in his face, but the man was serious. She later saw the posters on every billboard in town: WEAR RUBY W. GARTERS. The man even named the garters after her.

She liked to see the posters with her legs. But she didn't like the man. He made whistling sounds when he ate, and he talked in the middle of the night about his wife, Oriole.

Ruby was alone with Carrie one night. They sat in the parlor together and drank a great deal of Nicki's wine. Then Ruby thought of Karl. She wanted to see him. She took the beaded bag and her worn-out fur coat and her blue silk scarf and walked down past the Strassburg Furniture Store. Her scarf floated behind her like a breeze. She was strangely lovely as she walked unsteadily on her high, narrow heels, and she didn't look at anyone.

She swayed unsteadily outside the window of the

store. Dora was in the shop with Karl, and Ruby could see that she was going to have a baby. Dora didn't look pretty any more. She was swollen all over. Ruby stared at her fascinated, and then she pulled her fur coat around her and walked off.

She lunched uptown again, through the park and sat alone in the darkness. Karl had followed her there.

"If you could only understand—" There was something so broken in his voice, so pathetic. But she didn't answer him.

"Ruby—I've been miserable!"

They sat together a long time in the still and shadowy park. Karl clasped her hand tightly, and she could feel the sharp points of his nails on her skin.

"Ruby—remember the first time I met you?"

She closed her eyes, and heard again the song they heard together that first afternoon in the park. It was something so far away, almost forgotten, now.

"Ruby—Ruby—I'll always love you!" He crushed her blue scarf to his mouth, then he broke down completely:

"What's the use of living the way I do? I'm not making Dora happy—I'm not happy! Ruby, can't we be together again?"

He wanted to begin things again—and it was no use. She pulled her scarf around her neck and stumbled to her feet. She laughed. It was a husky laugh, and it rumbled in her throat.

When she got home, Nicki was there. She lurched past him, her blue scarf trailing on the floor. He picked it up and put it around her throat again.

"What's the matter, Ruby? Where you go so late like this?"

"In the park, Nick."

She stumbled to her room, and tried to unlock the door. She swayed drunkenly, and fell against Nicki. And then she laughed. It was the same strange laugh that Karl had heard.

"Sh-h! Baby—Carrie is asleep!"

He put his hand over her mouth and tried to still her laughter. She looked at him vaguely, and then she dropped her head. Her blue scarf fell to the floor again. She looked at it curiously, but she didn't pick it up.

"What's the matter? Tell Nicki."

She swayed unsteadily again. He caught her and held her for a moment.

"Give Nicki the key, baby—he will open door for you."

Her listless hands dropped the key to the floor. He picked it up quickly, and unlocked the door. She fell in a heap, and her rumpled hair hid her face entirely. Nicki sat down beside her and unloosened her coat.

"I want talk with you, Ruby."

"No, Nick—no."

"Nicki want to tell you so many things in his heart."

"No—not tonight."

"Why you love so many men—and you have no love—nothing for Nicki?"

"Don't love anyone."

"Yes, Ruby—you no get fur coat for nothing—you no get blue scarf for nothing—you no get this bag, shoes, for nothing."

"Sure—for nothing."

"Answer me, Ruby—tell me something—"

She tried to raise her head and look at him.

"Nicki give you better things than these. Nicki got lots of money. Tell Nicki what you want—he buy it for you."

She didn't answer him. She had hardly heard what he said. Then Nicki asked her to marry him.

She looked at him now through blurred eyes, and started to laugh again. She couldn't help thinking of Karl—Karl.

"We get married tonight—Ruby."

She put a hand to her head to clear away its blurred ache. The idea of marriage appealed to her.

"Sure, Nicki—sure."

Nicki tightened her fur coat around her, and tied her blue scarf around her hair. "We go quick—before Carrie hear."

He led her out. She watched him as he put out the lights. Then he took her out to his car. She fell against the seat. She was too drunk—too dazed, to care where they were going.

He drove her to a Judge's house, and he put a gold band on her finger. The Judge looked at them curiously. He had never married a beautiful drunken girl with pale gold hair to a Greek whose smile seemed painted and strange.

They drove back to the hat shop. Ruby was sober now. When Nicki took her in his arms and tried to hold her to him, she drew away and looked at him with contempt.

"Get out of my way, you big wop!"

She opened her door quickly, and locked herself in her room. Nicki tried to get in. Carrie tried to get in. Later, Ruby heard Carrie slopping around outside and pleading with Nicki. Ruby could only think that now Karl was gone forever.

Chapter XXXII

THE next morning she left the house as if she were coming back. She didn't. She picked up a fellow who was driving out of town. He left her at a country hotel. She had no money—nothing but her beaded bag, her blue scarf and her high heeled slippers, and her tight satin dress. She had left the fur coat for Carrie.

She took a job in the hotel as a waitress. She hated it. She hated carrying heavy trays and working around in the hot kitchen, listening to the cheap remarks of the cook.

None of the other waitresses bothered with Ruby. They didn't like her sullen manner. They were jealous of her indolent walk and her yellow hair. They didn't like the way she stopped her work and tried to hear the songs the young Russian played on his violin. They didn't like the young Russian either. He wore old suits and he couldn't talk English very well. He spoke with a deep, guttural sound, and it made the girls laugh. He was silent and aloof, and he never left large tips. He wasn't like the other men who came to the hotel.

Ruby was sitting outside the kitchen washing her hair and humming one of his songs in her low voice.

When he heard her he came down and sat beside her, and invited her to come to his room.

She sat on his bed and heard him play, and there was rapture on her face. His music vibrated through the room like something magic. It throbbed through her blood. It was elusive and bewildering, and half mad with a brilliant quality she had only heard on her victrola.

Later he heard her try to sing the melody. She was sitting on the porch in back of the hotel and drying her hair. The young Russian asked her to sing it over for him.

"I don't know nothin' about music!"

"I think you know very much."

"I don't know nothin' about it."

"You say so—but I know. With feeling it comes from your heart."

"I liked that song you played."

"Yes? Then I will play it again for you. You will sing it for me."

She sang the song in her husky voice. The tones were full and throbbing, and he thought she had a rare, plaintive quality. He wanted to hear her again. There was something haunting in her voice. Once, in his own country, he had heard a voice like that. She was a Gypsy, and sat on the side of the road in the dust and sang for money. Later she became a great singer. A passerby had discovered her.

CHAPTER XXXIII

NICKI came to the hotel one Sunday afternoon with Carrie, looking for his wife. He hadn't changed one bit. He still wore his brilliant shirts and oiled his hair.

"Why you run away like this—tell me?"

"I don't want to talk about that, Nick."

"Sure, you talk about it—that's why I come here."

"Then you better go back."

"You are my wife."

"I was drunk. I didn't know what I did."

"Sure you know—damn well!"

He picked up his suit case.

"Where your room, baby? I came this time to stay."

"You ain't goin' to stay, Nick."

"Sure, I am, Ruby. I wait helluva long time for chance like this."

Nothing had changed between Carrie and Nicki. They still lived in that room beyond the parlor with Carrie's pink lingerie, and Carrie's broad pillows, and Carrie's painted bed.

But Nicki wasn't Carrie's any more. He talked of Ruby all through the long night, and Carrie couldn't sleep. He had broken her spirit through those weeks when he talked of nothing but Ruby.

Nicki had tortured her during the ride to the hotel—the same thing over and over—Ruby. He would bring Ruby back to St. Marks, and he would rent the flat over the fruit store for her. He would buy new furniture at the Strassburg Furniture Store. He would put Ruby in that flat, and he would buy her things—shoes with bright bows, petticoats with ruffles, dresses of fine silk. He would show her off in his fruit store. He would make her sit by the counter and smile at his friends. Ruby would never get away from him again.

Carrie listened, and hated Ruby more than ever.

But Ruby's plans didn't fit in with Nicki's.

"I ain't goin' back, Nick."

His dream of the flat crumbled. "I marry you, Ruby. You are my wife."

"I ain't goin' back, Nick."

He couldn't bear her calmness. It almost maddened him. He struck her across her mouth. She said nothing, but faced him coldly. Like Carrie, he was afraid of her calmness. It licked him completely. He began to realize that she was beyond his reach and it maddened him.

He tried to hit her again, but Carrie stopped him. She was afraid that they would start something unpleasant at the hotel. She had seen what she wanted to know—Ruby would never live with Nicki—and now she was ready to take him back to St. Marks. She saw that Nicki might come back to her after all.

"Let's get out of here, Nick." She picked up his suit case, put on his hat and fixed his tie, and led him away.

But he didn't want to go. "I break her neck! Let me go back!"

She tried to make him get into the car. He pushed her away.

"Why you no leave me alone?"

She looked around anxiously. Many people were beginning to stare at them. "Everybody's lookin' at us. Come on—let's get out of here!"

He turned and said murderously: "I kill everybody in this place! Nicki not afraid!"

He took a step forward. Carrie rushed after him.

"You fool! They'll put you in jail! That's what they'll do!"

But Nicki didn't care about that. He started toward the onlookers on the porch. Then he stopped. A large man was coming toward him from the crowd.

"Come on, Nicki—come on."

Carrie was frantic.

Nicki turned with an oath and got into the car. He swung it around viciously and they drove away.

Chapter XXXIV

THEY went back to St. Marks. Carrie took him to the room beyond the parlor and poured him many a drink. He drank to heal his wounded pride. Carrie put her arms around him and rubbed his hair. He closed his eyes and drank some more. Carrie was glad to see him drink. It would make him forget.

But Nicki couldn't forget. Carrie's soothing hands, her soothing words, they could not make him forget.

"I go back for her—she no make fool out of me!"

He pushed Carrie's arms from his neck, and he started to talk incoherently. Carrie watched him, and through her muddled brain there ran one thought—she must never let him go back to Ruby.

They sat together far into the night. The wine had made him sob, and then turn vicious. Suddenly, he staggered to his feet. He was going back to get Ruby! He had married her! He had done what no one else had done—he had married her!

He started blindly for the door. Carrie clung to him, but he threw her against the wall. The sight of her made him crazy. She ran after him:

"She don't want you! Ruby hates you!"

But he didn't listen to her.

"No—she come back with me. I go kill her, Carrie. I go kill her!"

He said the words over and over. And he stumbled out into the street. She followed him.

"You can't go back!"

"Yes—I kill her! I kill her, Carrie!"

She walked beside him, and there was something so grim about her face. She almost smiled when she said to him:

"Sure, you're right, Nicki! Go back! Go back and kill her!"

He nodded his head and mumbled over and over:

"I kill her, all right."

He lurched on through the wet, dark streets. She took his arm. The harshness in his voice softened and he started to whimper like a beaten dog:

"I want her, Carrie—I want her! I no want to kill her!"

Carrie held his arm tightly. Her face was set. She was never going to let him go back to Ruby. They walked together down the street, across to the tracks.

Carrie had a plan.

A train was coming toward them. Nicki stumbled along, so helplessly drunk, he couldn't get out of the way. She held on to his arm desperately, and her face was passive and dead.

Just one push and he would never go back to Ruby. Then she started to sob bitterly. She loved Nicki. She couldn't do this to him.

"Come on back!" She jerked him toward her. They both stumbled to the side of the road. He fell beside her in the grass, and started to whimper again.

Silently, Carrie watched the train go by, and she was glad she hadn't pushed him.

"Come on, Nick—let's go home."

"I want her, Carrie. She is so beautiful!"

He said the words in a thick voice and they cut her like a knife. She took his hand and dragged him up and along the tracks. He followed her blindly. He didn't know what was going through Carrie's dull, hazy mind.

"I want her, Carrie."

"Sure, I know—I know what you mean." She dragged him after her for a long time. Then suddenly she became frightened as no train appeared.

At last she heard the shrill whistle. The train was rushing toward them. He would never go back to Ruby now. She set her mouth and pushed him.

He fell on the tracks like a rag. Carrie turned, stumbling back over the long tracks to the hat shop.

It was all over now. She felt very calm, as though Nicki wasn't dead at all. In her room, she picked up his ties and his shirts—his old belt. She put them away in the closet beside her things. Slowly—slowly, she began to realize that she had killed him. Frightened and bewildered, she started to moan. It was a terrible moan.

The next day she sat in her chair in the window and made hats as if nothing had happened.

Then, one day, they sold Nicki's store to a bakery, and took off his sign from the window. That was when she realized that even his name had vanished now.

That was the day she burned his old ties, and his shirts, and his belt. It was no use keeping them in her closet any more.

Chapter XXXV

Ruby came back. Carrie told her that Nicki was dead. He had fallen before a train, was drunk that night—the night Ruby wouldn't come back to St. Marks with him.

Ruby was free of him now. She was packing her bags—going away from St. Marks forever.

Carrie watched her leave. Ruby carried her battered suit case and was swinging her beaded bag. Carrie watched her out of sight. She knew Ruby would never come back. She also knew that she was glad. She was glad, too, that Ruby didn't know she had killed Nicki because he wanted to push her out of his life.

The young Russian was waiting for Ruby at the station. They got on the train together. They were going to New York.

He had a career in New York. He played for a cafe. And Ruby—Ruby would study music. He had told her there was beauty in her low throaty voice. There was a deep emotional quality that needed to be trained. But she must study hard. She must start and build it carefully and painstakingly. She listened.

They sat together in the worn, velvet seat of the train, and they were both silent. Slowly, slowly, they passed through the town where Ruby had lived. Slowly, slowly, back of shops, back of restaurants— slowly, past the Strassburg Furniture Store with the gold sign—and then quickly out of town to the wooded parts.

He touched her hand:

"You'll be glad you leave this place. You'll be glad you go to New York. Everyone begins life in New York. It's the only way."

She looked at his sensitive face, and she smiled vaguely.

The train rushed on. Ruby watched the sign boards. There were so many posters of a pair of woman's legs in sheer, black hose, held up by a pair of blue satin garters. The posters read: WEAR RUBY W. GARTERS.

The sign followed the train for miles and miles. She remembered the man who drew those legs. She remembered the funny whistle in his mouth when he ate.

She wondered if Boris knew the legs belonged to her. But he didn't know it, and she was glad. Soon the signs were left behind; she would never see them again. That part of her life was gone. She was going away. She was going to be something. Boris had told her of the Gypsy woman who sat in the road and sang in a throbbing voice like Ruby's. The Gypsy woman had become a great singer.

She pushed the corn-colored hair away from her forehead, and she leaned back against the velvet seat.

"I'm goin' to be somethin'—I'll learn, all right. I'll be somethin'."

Her face was pale as ivory. Boris kissed her gently. She closed her eyes and thought of Karl—Karl. . . .

It was many years later that Karl left his family certain nights of the week, and went alone to his furniture store. His mother was curious. She came upon him unaware one night. The store was dark. She could see the outline of Karl's figure hunched in a chair, his head buried in his hands. He was listening to a glorious voice that came from the radio. The beauty of the tone fascinated Mrs. Strassburg, too. She stood and listened. Then walked silently to her son and sat beside him.

"Listen to her, ma—listen!"

The voice floated in beauty, rose in a brilliant crescendo and then died. Then followed a loud acclaim of applause.

"Such a beautiful voice, Karl."

There was a look of ecstasy in his face.

"I told her she would be something some day—I told her."

Mrs. Strassburg was stunned for a moment. She

understood.

"That girl, Karl—that girl?"

He nodded. "Ruby. She sings in concert now. She was a great success in New York. I read she's going to Europe next fall."

Mrs. Strassburg sighed and stroked her son's head.

"You should be happy you married Dora, Karl. You have two fine children—you are rich—Dora has been a good wife, Karl."

He smiled.

Then Karl took his hat and left the store. He thought over what his mother had said. He was rich. He had two fine children. He walked through the streets, past the Empire Hotel, over to the park. He sat a long time on their bench. Ruby's and his! He closed his eyes, and heard her glorious voice again. He whispered her name: "Ruby—" Then a warm feeling crept into his heart. For the first time in all these years he began to think he was glad he had given her up—glad he had married Dora. For Ruby had become something finer—greater—than marriage to him could ever have made of her.

It was very late when he finally went home to Dora.

THE END

www.ingramcontent.com/pod-product-compliance
Lightning Source LLC
Chambersburg PA
CBHW061611100726
47898CB00002B/615